The Wells Fargo

Gold Rush

The Wells Fargo Book of the Gold Rush

by *Margaret Rau*

Illustrations from the Wells Fargo Historical Archives

ATHENEUM BOOKS FOR YOUNG READERS
NEW YORK   LONDON   TORONTO   SYDNEY   SINGAPORE

Acknowledgments

I would like to express my gratitude to Dr. Robert Chandler of Wells Fargo Historical Services for his valuable assistance in my research; to John Gonzales of the California State Library for his valuable aid; and to Kate McGinn at the Henry E. Huntington Library for hers. I would also like to thank all the librarians in the Santa Barbara Library, the Sacramento City Library, and the San Francisco City Library for their help in locating necessary materials for the book.

Atheneum Books for Young Readers
An imprint of Simon & Schuster Children's Publishing Division
1230 Avenue of the Americas
New York, New York 10020

Book design by Debbie Sfetsios
The text of this book is set in Adobe Caslon.
Printed in the United States of America

2 4 6 8 10 9 7 5 3 1

Library of Congress Cataloging-in-Publication Data
Rau, Margaret.
The Wells Fargo book of the gold rush / by Margaret Rau ;
illustrations from the Wells Fargo archives.—1st ed.
      p.   cm.
Summary: Chronicles the California gold rush, from its beginning in 1848,
through its peak, to the 1849 recession that brought about its end.
ISBN 0-689-83019-X
1. California—Gold discoveries—Pictorial works—Juvenile literature. 2. California—History—
1846–1850—Pictorial works—Juvenile literature. 3. Frontier and pioneer life—California—
Pictorial works—Juvnile literature. [1. California—Gold discoveries.
2. California—History—1846–1850.] I. Wells, Fargo & Company. II. Title.
F865.R28 2000
979.4'04—dc21   99-028767

FIRST
EDITION

Contents

Introduction

"This is the worst place to live in I ever saw. The people are all thieves and cutthroats except *me* and my *husband*," a San Franciscan wrote. Just what sort of a destination was this strange land called California?

Read Margaret Rau's lively narrative for a tumultuous tale that turned a distant Mexican province into the melting pot of the world.

"You know when a fellow is through with his day's work, he has got to bake a loaf or wash the dishes or cut wood, and when Sunday comes, there is a half dozen dirty shirts to wash or else go to town for some grub. That is the way my leisure hours go." That was "leisure"?

What was work? Look at 1850s illustrations, drawn from such California publications as the *Annals of San Francisco* and *Hutching's California Magazine.*

"We went mining and Mary got some four dollars out of three pans of dirt. If you could have seen her eyes stick out when she saw the first piece, about *4 cents worth*. She thought she had a fortune."

Is this a true picture of mining life? Enjoy Margaret Rau's descriptions to find out.

Perhaps stooping in icy streams is not for you? Why not, instead, enjoy cultured San Francisco, rated now one of the finest cities of the world? Well, maybe conditions have changed in one hundred and fifty years:

"It is cold here nights as Greenland—" (a San Franciscan wrote on July 28) "—It is a beautiful morning until 10 o'clock, then you imagine the wind blowing and the dust a flying enough to take the breath out of us. Hoops and ankles, leg exhibited all for nothing. Oh, this is the spot to see pretty feet. It affords the gaffers good amusement through the afternoon. When bed time comes, we amuse ourselves with catching *Fleas*. After this, we can sleep as sweet dreamers under 2 pairs of thick blankets, until the sun shines in upon us so hot that it forces us out of this."

Possibly four-star lodging was not too plentiful. Discover what Margaret Rau has to say!

"There is not a day that passes, but what I think of home. I never lie down at night without thinking of home and friends, but the idea of going home without money at the age at which I have arrived; to live upon the bounty of others, is more than I can do. This living upon excitement, in sinking deep holes, moving from place to place hoping and expecting, that will injure the strongest constitution, or the strongest mind."

Did Californians go around continually in a state of depression?

Henry Wells did not think so. On a visit in 1853, he declared, "This is a great country and a greater people." Wells did something about it, too. He joined fellow New Yorker William George Fargo to form a financial institution that has served California—and the nation—since 1852. After all, miners did find gold.

"7th, Put horse on ranch; 9th, Commence mining; 10th, $14; 11th, $21.10; 12th, $14.50; 13th, $12.40; 14th, $11.70; 15th, Sunday, rote letter," a miner jotted in his pocket diary.

What did gold seekers do with treasure? They carefully husbanded funds for living expenses and to send to their loved ones at home. In those gold rush days, Wells, Fargo & Co., Banking and Express, provided financial, delivery, and letter services. To celebrate the Golden State's sesquicentennial, Wells Fargo is pleased to support Margaret Rau's tale of gold!

Dr. Robert J. Chandler, Ph.D.
HISTORICAL SERVICES
WELLS FARGO

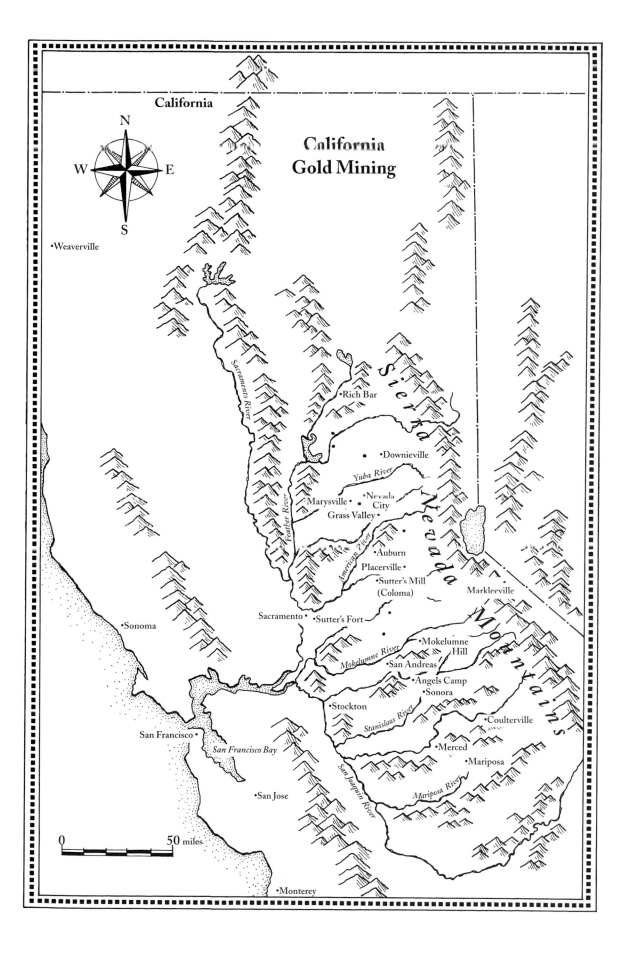

The Wells Fargo Book of the Gold Rush

Eureka! Gold!

ON THE MORNING OF JANUARY 24, 1848, JAMES Marshall was making his usual early-morning inspection of the ditch his men had been digging the day before, part of the sawmill Marshall was building. Once lumbering operations began, the ditch, known as a tailrace, would carry away the debris and dump it into the river below the mill.

Suddenly Marshall halted his casual inspection, his attention caught by a glittering flake among the pebbles in the bed of the tailrace. He stopped to get a closer look. Was it gold, or just iron pyrites masquerading as gold? Probably the latter, Marshall thought. For years there had been false rumors of gold in the Mexican-owned province of California. But few specimens had proved to be more than trace minerals, if that. Just to be sure, Marshall began looking around. There were other flakes he saw now, washed down the tailrace by the water with which they had scoured it.

Marshall began gathering the flakes. All around him the wakening day filled the chilly mountain valley, casting a shawl of glassy light upon the stands of sugar pine that would presently provide ready material for the sawmill. Over all was the sound of water rushing down the South Fork of the American

Thirty-five-year-old James Marshall, a carpenter by trade, became both a trusted employee and loyal friend of Captain John Sutter. It was Marshall who launched the gold rush.

Guarded by the towering Sierra Nevada range, the rugged foothills, a land of rushing streams and wooded slopes, concealed a treasure in gold waiting to be discovered.

River, on its way to its union with the Sacramento River in the valley below.

These were the foothills of the Sierra Nevada range that, like a lofty spine, rose between California and the territory of Nevada. Marshall had little appreciation for the beauty of this small mountain valley, which the local Native Americans called "Coloma," meaning "beautiful view." He was here on a mission to find the perfect spot for the sawmill he was building for his employer and friend, John Sutter.

Sutter was a Swiss adventurer. He had traveled around the world launching dream after dream only to see each one collapse. In 1839 he had come to California, which then was a province of Mexico, where he planned to launch his last venture. He was convinced that this one would succeed. He had no problem obtaining a grant from Juan Bautista Alvarado, the alcalde, or governor, of the province with headquarters at Monterey. Alvarado was a generous man who liked Sutter's idea of starting a colony in a wilderness area of California, and granted him some fifty-five thousand acres of land. They lay on the fork of the American River where it joined the Sacramento River.

Sutter called the estate New Helvetia, giving it Switzerland's ancient name. He built an adobe fort on a rise of ground to oversee his vast holdings. He purchased equipment from the Russians, who were closing their trading station, Fort Ross, which stood some ninety miles north of San Francisco. Sutter's purchases included farming and tanning equipment, horses, mules, carts and wagons, a forge, a gristmill, even a twenty-ton schooner, along with bells, some old cannon, and plenty of ammunition.

Already short of cash, Sutter went heavily into debt to the Russians. He hoped to recoup his losses once his operation was going. Meanwhile, he mounted the cannons on top of his fort, strung up his bells, and set up the gristmill. He built a slaughterhouse and a workshop for the forge, and another for the tanning operations. Because he had good grazing grounds, he brought in three thousand head of cattle. And because the soil was fertile and conditions were just right, he planted wheat and orchards. He employed Native Americans to work his land. Observers claimed they were actually slaves. It was not unusual among California ranchers of that day to use the native people this way. And Sutter needed a cheap source of labor. Most of his life he had lived on a shoestring, financing his extravagant lifestyle on credit. This time, he reasoned, he would surely be successful.

Sutter had some uncertainty about his holdings when, in 1847, war broke out between the United States and Mexico. It had ended with a quick defeat of Mexico and the ceding of California to the United States. Sutter wondered if his grant

John Sutter, a Swiss adventurer, dreamed of establishing his own little barony in California.

**The beautiful Coloma valley on the South Fork of the American River
was the site on which Marshall chose to build a sawmill. Coloma had the
two requirements needed—thick stands of trees and a rapid stream.**

would be canceled by the new regime. He was relieved to learn that the United
States would honor all holders of grants, whether they were Americans, Mexicans,
or other nationalities.

Sutter was free to continue developing his property. One of his first needs
was a sawmill. The closest obtainable lumber for his building plans now had to
come from San Francisco at tremendous cost. With his own sawmill Sutter
could supply not only his needs but also those of other settlers in the valley.

This was why he had sent his trusted employee and friend, James Marshall,
a skilled carpenter, to locate a suitable spot for the mill. Now, staring at the
glimmering flakes he held, Marshall thought that if this really was gold and
Sutter could lay first claim on the surrounding land, all his monetary worries
would vanish.

Sutter had to be told at once. That night, after work on the sawmill was ended for the day, Marshall saddled his horse and set off in a sudden blinding rainstorm. Sliding over muddy patches, he rode at breakneck speed down the treacherous trail to the fort. It was well past midnight by the time he arrived.

Marshall's loud shouts awakened an alarmed Sutter, who rushed out to see what the problem was. By the dim light of a lantern, Marshall showed him the glimmering flakes. Wide awake now, Sutter began testing Marshall's find. Over and over he repeated the tests. When he had finished, he looked at Marshall. In an awed voice he gave his opinion.

"Gold, the finest kind of gold."

The two men stared at each other, realizing that speed and secrecy were both important now. If word got out that gold had been found in quantity, there would be a mad stampede to the site. Immediately they formed a partnership and made their plans. First they had to lay claim to the area where Marshall had found the gold. And they had to do it before word leaked out. If they were successful in this, they would hold between them an extraordinary fortune and Sutter would be free to fulfill his dream of becoming a kind of feudal baron, ruling over his own little kingdom, New Helvetia, sustained by an everlasting hoard of gold!

A City Is Created

ARLY THE NEXT MORNING SUTTER ACCOMPANIED Marshall to Coloma. There he sought out the chiefs of the neighboring tribe, a farming community, who claimed this land as their ancestral home. From them he secured a lease to work the land, paying the chiefs with clothing, some farm tools, and a pledge to grind their wheat free of charge in the new flour mill he hoped to build with the lumber that would be floated from the sawmill downstream to Sutter's Fort. Useful articles in exchange for a chance to collect worthless golden dust? To the chiefs this was a great deal.

Sutter had his lease, but he realized he was still on uncertain ground. He decided to register a further claim in Monterey, choosing Charles Bennett as his emissary. Carrying a packet of gold dust, which Sutter hoped would convince the government to grant his claim and thereby prevent a mad stampede, Bennett set off.

He was to discover that the governor was no longer the friendly Mexican alcalde with whom Sutter had dealt. Since California was now a United States possession, it was being governed by the United States military forces, though still using Mexico's form of government. Colonel Richard B. Mason was the new alcalde. He was brusque and matter-of-fact. Everyone knew that California had no gold. It was a well-established fact. Bennett was turned away empty-handed.

A gold seeker burdened with the necessary equipment heads for the
gold fields.

Though Mason had refused Bennett's request, rumors of a rich gold strike on the South Fork of the American River had started floating around San Francisco. By April, a small number of curious San Franciscans began traveling to the South Fork to do a little digging themselves.

One of these visitors was Sam Brannan, a former elder of the Mormon Church. Brannan had come to San Francisco in 1846 and opened a supply house there. He had done a lot of his business with Sutter's Fort.

On one of his trips to the fort, Brannan visited the diggings and saw with his own eyes how rich they were. Around the middle of May he returned to San Francisco, brimming with excitement. Holding high a glass bottle containing gleaming gold dust, he began rushing up and down San Francisco's muddy streets, shouting at the top of his voice, "Gold! Gold! Gold! A bonanza of gold on the South Fork. Gold!"

Some say Brannan wanted to get a gold rush going so he could open a supply store at Coloma. Others said it was just Sam acting in his usual exuberant manner.

Throngs of ships in San Francisco Bay were left unattended to rot away as their captains and crews joined the mad rush for the gold fields.

Whatever the reason, Brannan's delirious spectacle was the spark that set San Francisco afire. And the gold rush of 1848 was on. Carpenters left their jobs, deserting unfinished buildings. Clerks fled their desks. The new schoolhouse lost its teacher. Even members of the town council joined the rush.

There was a run on shops selling everything from shovels and picks to bowie knives and flat-bottomed bowls. When the shelves were empty, the shopkeepers closed their doors and joined the rush. Only one blacksmith stayed behind. He was making a good profit pounding out picks for the new prospectors.

The fever spread to the military. American soldiers stationed at the presidio left in a body, galloping away on the horses reserved for their officers. Navy men as well as soldiers headed for the gold fields. Merchant ships coming into harbor were deserted by crews and captains who were all heading for the South Fork, leaving their empty ships behind to rot in the bay.

By the end of May the fever had reached Monterey. Soon all the servants at the governor's mansion had vanished, leaving him to prepare his own meals and ponder his dismissal of Bennett.

Gold! Gold! Gold! Streams paved with it! The word spread northward and southward. Soon all California was on the move. That summer and fall, throngs of gold seekers trekked through the California valleys toward the American River and its tributaries. All along the way unscrupulous travelers stole cattle and horses from ranches, and broke down fences enclosing fields of ripening wheat. Sometimes they left smoldering campfires behind. In the hot, dry

The early miners needed little equipment to pan for gold: a pan with a flat bottom, a pickax to claw gold out of the crevices, and a shovel to scoop up dirt and debris and dump it into the pan. One other necessity—water—would come from a nearby stream.

weather, some of the embers ignited the wheat and fields burst into flame, leaving behind a blackened earth. The sky became heavy with a stifling haze.

And still the throngs of gold seekers continued on. They came to Sutter's Fort on their journey to the mountains, but Sutter was having problems. Most of his paid workers had quit to get a turn at the gold. His native crew had reaped the wheat and left. There was no one to thresh it. The tanners were all gone, leaving a thousand cattle hides to rot.

At first, Sutter was able to keep afloat by selling quantities of supplies to the prospectors who were streaming by his fort. But merchants drawn by the wonderful opportunity to sell to all these people had begun establishing branch stores along the Sacramento River on Sutter's property, claiming squatters' rights. The merchants were followed by small ramshackle boardinghouses, saloons, gambling dens, shoddy eating houses.

The young town of Sacramento as it appeared in 1849, shortly after John Sutter's son sold lots on part of his father's holdings to pay off the older man's heavy debts.

The stream of prospectors began spilling over onto the compound around the fort. It was soon filled with ragged, grimy men, with horses, mules, wagons, supply barrels containing all kinds of merchandise. There was no way to control the rabble. Round-the-clock drinking and gambling went on. Fierce quarrels broke out, some ending in murder. And there were no police to bring an end to the violence.

"They stole the cattle and the horses," Sutter complained bitterly to friends. "They stole my barrels of supplies. They stole the bells from the fort and the weights from the gates."

But Sutter blamed what he considered his last indignity on his young son, John Sutter. Hearing of his father's predicament, the twenty-two-year-old Sutter rushed to his father's side to learn that the older man was being inundated by a mountain of debt. To keep him from losing everything, young Sutter made the only move possible: He divided some of his father's holdings along the Sacramento River into city lots and sold them at a good price. The lots were snatched up quickly, both by merchants and by private individuals wanting to build homes there.

With the money he received, young Sutter was able to pay off his father's debts, but the old man never forgave him for destroying his dream of a New Helvetia. With a jaundiced eye he watched a new town, the town of Sacramento, spring up on land that had once been his.

Meanwhile, 1848 was drawing to a close. California had passed through the first surge of the gold rush. But it was far from over. The year of the forty-niners would soon be on its way. And it would see the wildest, dizziest rush yet to the land of gold.

Forty-Niners by Land

ON DECEMBER 8, 1848, JAMES KNOX POLK, PRESIDENT of the United States of America, attached Colonel Mason's report from California to his message to Congress. That report set off a reaction that almost destroyed the economic stability of the young United States. The report read, "Recent discoveries render it probable that these mines are more extensive and valuable than was anticipated."

The report seemed to be proved conclusively by the container of glimmering golden flakes on display at the war office for all who wished to see.

Gold! Gold! Gold! The news spread with the speed of lightning. Papers picked up the sober report and embellished it with wild stories of rivers of gold, meadows covered with grass whose roots clutched nuggets of gold. Under every rock, according to some reports, lay a million-dollar hoard of gold just waiting to be discovered. The wilder the stories, the greater the excitement.

Suddenly a great swell of movement westward began. Thousands of farmers from the frontier lands of the Midwest were preparing to leave the farms they had wrested from the wilderness at such great effort to journey to the land of gold. They brought out the large wagons that had in former years carried them here, and once again covered them with canvas stretched on hoops to create covered wagons. Then they piled the wagons high with as many belongings as they would hold.

The long parade of forty-niners, wagon after wagon, makes its way
across miles of wilderness to answer the call of gold.

Provisions came first, and so in went bags of flour, eggs packed in sawdust,
bacon and salt pork, vegetables if they had them. They packed frying pans, pots
and kettles, water buckets and firearms, ropes, axes, picks, lanterns, blankets and
changes of clothing, medicine chests containing simple family remedies. Some
brought furniture, musical instruments, even small libraries. Several brought
gold-washing machines created by inventors who knew nothing about mining
for placer gold.

Wagons packed, teams hitched, reserve horses, mules, and oxen herded into
formation, off they set. The meeting places were frontier towns on the Missouri
River—Saint Joseph or Independence. Most of the travelers were young unmarried men. But there were some heads of families who were leaving their wives
and children behind to mind the farm in their absence. And a few were taking
their wives and children along, with the thought that if they liked the country,

perhaps they would take up farming there. All of them expected to make a quick garnering of gold after which they would return to their former lives.

Before setting out, they formed into companies made up mostly of friends and relatives. Each company drew up its own rules. They were almost identical—no quarreling, no drinking, no gambling, no profanity, no labor on the Sabbath. Finally, each member was required to take a solemn vow to help any other member who might need it.

At last the companies were ready to set out. One behind the other, thousands of covered wagons rolled into the broad prairie lands that stretched away westward. They were now traveling through the lands of the Sioux. They had been warned of hostile Indians, but they had no serious threat from them, though there were numerous pilferings.

Single men, and even some females with small children, joined the long trek westward. Unmindful of the hazards that would face them, they were drawn by the irresistible lure of gold.

One after another, the covered wagons roll westward across the prairies, over mountains and through deserts, leaving behind the picked-clean skeletons of overworked oxen that had dropped in their tracks.

During those first days the journey seemed like a lark. The lush green prairie grass provided food for the animals. And herds of buffalo feeding in the distance awakened the urge of the hunters among the travelers. They vied with one another to see how many of the great beasts they could bring down. Behind them they left a trail of shaggy carcasses marked overhead by circling vultures.

But even before they reached Fort Kearney, Wyoming, their troubles began. The loaded wagons were already tiring the teams of oxen. Winter rains had pockmarked the prairies with hidden bog holes in which the oxen became mired. The wagons had to be unloaded to lighten them, and the weary animals urged out of the muck. Then the wagons had to be reloaded before the column could move forward. This meant long delays.

Beyond Fort Kearney the trail became rougher as prairies gave way to jumbled rock formations. The weakened teams could hardly make the gently rising ascent that led into the Rocky Mountains. Reluctantly the forty-niners began tossing out their excess baggage to make things easier for the animals. The trail behind them became littered with chairs, stoves, trunks, quilts, even tools and firearms. Next came food—bags of flour and bags of beans, quarters of ham and great slabs of bacon. Even then some of the limping oxen died in their harness. Their discarded carcasses joined the scattered luggage.

The crippled procession struggled on, up the slopes of the Rockies, through South Pass, then down the western slopes. Beyond the mountain range the trail wound through more tumbled land on its way to the valley of the Great Salt Lake. Rivers rushing from the high mountains had to be crossed. Mormons who had settled in these parts operated ferry boats at the crossings, but the ferries only carried wagons. Men and animals had to get across on their own, and since most of the travelers couldn't swim, many drowned. Many others suffered from another scourge—cholera, which periodically plagued the camps. Pneumonia was another great killer. And there were accidents with guns, some the result of flaring tempers.

Salt Lake City gave the forty-niners a respite. They replenished their dwindling food supplies and bought quantities of grass for their animals. Then they were on their way again—down the valley and up the steep canyons that threaded through the mountains, hemming in the western end of the valley.

Finally the forty-niners reached the greatest challenge of all—the wide empty desert lands that lay between them and the Sierra Nevada. For the first three hundred miles they followed the shallow, muddy Humboldt River. It didn't provide much grazing, but its water, muddy though it was, was vital to both animals and humans.

After the Humboldt dwindled away into a series of stagnant sinkholes, the caravan still had to cross fifty waterless miles before it reached the rivers that flowed out of the Sierra Nevada. That long, waterless trek had to be made under a blistering desert sun. The forty-niners forgot about gold. All they could think of now was how to survive until they reached water again.

Weak and dehydrated, humans and beasts staggered on. Only remnants of the initial mighty caravan finally reached the Carson River, where they camped and at last drank their fill of water.

Ahead of them now rose the towering Sierra Nevada, the final barrier to the gold that waited on the western slopes. Step after step the forty-niners urged themselves and their animals upward. Cattle faltered and dropped. Wagons tilted and spilled their last contents. Haggard and gaunt, the men pushed on, helping the struggling women and children.

Fortunately, the news of their plight had raced ahead of them, and a relief party was soon on its way. Trains of horses and mules arrived carrying provisions. Women and children were placed on the horses and escorted over the mountains to the nearest settlements. The straggling companies of men and animals, now fed and watered, found new strength and spirits. They had made it. They had

Finally the caravan comes to the last long ascent over the Sierra Nevada. The telegraph lines were completed by 1861. The formidable Sierra Nevada was just one of the obstacles that divided eastern telegraph service from western telegraph service.

reached the land of gold and plenty at last. Yet their triumph must have been tempered by the haunting memory of lost friends and companions lying in lonely unmarked graves along that never-ending trail.

Forty-Niners by Sea

PEOPLE LIVING ON THE EAST COAST OF THE United States were just as excited as the frontier people. But they turned to the sea to get to the gold fields. By sea, they would have to travel to the southern tip of South America and then up the western coast of both South and North America to San Francisco, a distance of some ten thousand miles. It was impossible to judge how long the trip would take, because the sailing vessels depended on the vagaries of the wind and weather.

This meant the trip would be expensive. Passage alone would cost from $300 to $799, not including expenditures along the way. Doctors, lawyers, business and professional men of all kinds could draw the necessary money out of large bank accounts. Clerks on modest salaries had to risk their life savings, while farm boys mortgaged their farms.

Some groups of people pooled their resources to purchase an entire ship and fill its hold with merchandise that they thought would find a ready market in San Francisco, a small frontier town perched at the end of nowhere. Other young men were sponsored by their townships and were expected to reward this patronage with a percentage of the profits once they struck gold.

Only men were accepted aboard the first ships because, instead of private cabins, the sleeping quarters were dormitories crowded with tiers of bunks. The would-be travelers had numerous guidebooks put out to tell those headed for the gold fields

A clipper ship, fastest sails on the sea, bound for San Francisco by way of Cape Horn, takes on passengers and freight at an eastern port.

what they would need. Many had obviously been written by people who had never been to California. Some advised bringing nothing but cotton shirts and dungarees, Panama hats fitted with netting to ward off the mosquitoes, and umbrellas to protect from sunstroke. Others advised heavy woolen clothing and thick, rough overcoats that would have satisfied explorers heading for the North Pole. Others suggested gold mining items which included gold-washing machines, test tubes, and crucibles, and one guidebook even recommended bringing along a small cannon as protection against "hostile native tribes."

Burdened with these unnecessary belongings, young men by the thousands

An overcrowded dormitory on a ship bound for gold country.

hurried to the nearest seaport. By mid-January of 1849, one-fifth of the town of Plymouth, Massachusetts, had put to sea. And another thousand or so were waiting impatiently to board the next available ship. The demand was so great that some ships, arriving in eastern harbors with other destinations planned, canceled them and changed course for San Francisco. Shipyards went into high gear putting together new ships. Old ships ready to be scrapped were given superficial repairs to keep them afloat and were again put into service.

All of the ships were quickly filled with "Argonauts," as the gold seekers were called, after the legendary Jason, who set sail in his ship, the *Argo*, to find and bring home the mythical Golden Fleece.

Each shipload of Argonauts had its own unique experiences at sea, but they all followed the same general pattern. Since it was winter in the northern hemisphere, the first days out of New England ports were often boisterous ones. Passengers unused to sea travel, crowded together in airless holds, became so seasick that they were forced to take to their bunks.

As the ships moved southward the weather became calmer, and passengers were able to leave their bunks to stroll the decks. Many wrote passages in their diaries describing the enchanting coastal scenery and the varying moods of a playful sea.

But the climate changed yet again as the ships neared the equator. Warmth gave way to oppressive heat that drove the passengers from their stuffy dormitory to sleep on deck.

Sometimes when a ship crossed the equator, its captain would try to cheer his depressed passengers with a little ceremony. One of the sailors, dressed in green and carrying a trident, would clamber over the railings as Neptune, god of the sea. After some mild hazing to initiate the passengers on their first crossing of the equator, the captain would serve a sumptuous meal followed by toasts from the ship's store of brandy.

And still the ships sailed southward, stopping at ports along the way to replenish their supplies. There the passengers had a chance to stretch their legs ashore and marvel at the exotic architecture, food, and customs of a foreign country. But with every nautical mile southward, the days grew shorter and the weather colder, for it was autumn in the countries below the equator, where seasons are reversed. It would be winter by the time the ships reached treacherous Cape Horn, or "Cape Stiff," as the sailors called it.

All depended now on the winds to carry the ships through the narrow passageway ahead. The captains had two routes to choose from. One led through the Strait of Le Maire. It was the most southern of the straits. The northern passageway, the Strait of Magellan, cut hundreds of miles off the distance. But though it was shorter, it was also more dangerous. The currents were swift and the passageway was narrow, sometimes less than two miles wide.

Whichever route the ships chose, the passage around Cape Horn was full of danger. Clear days might at a moment's notice give way to fierce squalls of sleet and snow and wild winds that would toss the ship round and round. Unless a captain was very skillful at maneuvering his floundering ship, it could end up scudding into the jagged cliffs and desolate, rock-bound bays of Cape Stiff or the barren islands that clustered around it. Sometimes the passengers managed to make it ashore to be rescued by a following ship. But more often the ship and all aboard would go down together. There is no record of how many were lost in the perilous passage around Cape Stiff.

On the western side of Cape Horn the ships finally started the journey north toward California. A growing boredom now gripped the impatient passengers. At first they tried to find things to do to pass the time. Some spent hours rearranging the cargo in the ship's hold; others sewed leather containers to hold the caches of

Passengers making their way to San Francisco by way of the Isthmus of Panama covered the first leg of their sixty-mile trek from east to west by water.

gold treasure they expected to gather. During the course of the voyage, one passenger created fifteen such bags, each capable of holding twenty pounds of gold dust.

As contrary winds and becalmed seas ate into the hours and days, tempers grew short. Passengers began quarreling among themselves, and then joined together to complain about the captain. They griped about the monotonous meals of salt pork and hardtack, a tasteless bread made of flour and water without even salt to flavor it. They cursed the contrary winds, or lack of any wind at all. They wondered what malignant force was playing tricks on them and they moaned that all the gold would be gone before they even arrived.

Sometimes things didn't go smoothly.

Not all the Argonauts booked passage on sailing ships. By this time, little paddle steamers had begun plying coastal waters. They carried mail down the eastern coast of the United States to the Isthmus of Panama, where the mail was dispatched by courier across the isthmus to Panama City on the western coast. There another paddle steamer hurried the mail north to San Francisco.

The passengers who chose this route suffered their own brand of hardship. They had to cross the fifty or so miles of rugged tropical jungle that lay between the eastern and western coasts of the isthmus. Until a railroad was built, travel went partly by water, either by canoe or on worn-out steamboats that periodically broke down. Then there would be miles more to cover on mule and on foot, much of it along the tops of steep cliffs, where a single misstep could send the unwary plunging to death. In addition, there were bandits who lay in wait along this isolated stretch of road.

Even more dangerous than bandits were the tropical diseases that threatened the traveler: typhus, malaria, dysentery, dengue fever, typhoid, cholera. There was no relief for the travelers in Panama City. The hotels were usually full, and the

Overcrowded paddle steamers still stopped at Panama City for supplies on their way to San Francisco.

newcomers had to sleep on bare, soggy ground in crowded tents until the next coastal steamer arrived.

There was always a mad dash of marooned travelers to get aboard. Many had to be turned back from ships already seriously overcrowded. A traveler might have to stay in Panama for weeks, even months, before he was finally able to force his way aboard. Often a person with a contagious disease was among the passengers, and soon the whole ship was stricken with an epidemic. On the *Uncle Sam,* cholera broke out. One hundred four people from a passenger list of three hundred died and were buried at sea before the ship reached San Francisco Bay.

But whatever the circumstances, once a ship entered that narrow passageway that led to the bay, excitement swept like a fever through the passengers. They began making preparations for the final landing, rechecking their pistols, sharpening their knives, shovels, picks, and axes for the last time, and finally packing everything away. When they had things ready for disembarking, they dressed in their best outfits and began parading around the deck. And in that glow of success they even saw fit to praise the captain whose sterling qualities had brought them to this moment.

San Francisco

AS THE SHIP PASSED THROUGH THE NARROW channel and entered the harbor, the passengers stared in wonder. Before them lay a quiet, landlocked bay strewn with green islands. The mainland was a series of oak-crowned hills rolling upward into a hazy sky.

As the ship progressed, the Argonauts were amazed to see a dense forest of tall-masted ships crowding the waterfront. Almost all the ships were empty. An Argonaut who arrived in 1852 wrote, "These ships had a very old, ruinous, and antiquated appearance . . . gave me an impression that this newborn city had been inhabited for ages and was now going to ruin."

But the city was far from ruin. As soon as the ship rounded Clark's Point, a bevy of small boats suddenly began swarming across the bay to cluster around the new arrival. The boatmen all started shouting out offers to carry the bewildered Argonauts to shore, at three dollars a head.

The first ferries were joined by other boats. They arrived carrying agents from the town's auction houses. If the merchandise the ship was carrying included things that were in short supply, a din of bidding rose from various quarters. The bidders held up bags of gold dust as proof they were in earnest. To the Argonauts the bids seemed extravagantly high. It was their first introduction to the inflated prices of everything in San Francisco.

Sometimes the boats contained employers or their agents looking for carpenters,

The city soon found use for the abandoned ships in the harbor by turning them into hotels or warehouses.

blacksmiths, clerks, chefs, waiters. The wages they offered astonished the newcomers. One day's earnings could equal a whole week's wages back east. It was obvious that San Francisco was booming. The city that had been almost empty during the 1848 gold rush was now alive again, as the Argonauts discovered when they disembarked. People swarmed through the streets. Among the Californians were people from around the world, wearing different costumes, speaking different languages. Gold had brought them here—many had come not to search for gold but to sell merchandise to those who were arriving to dig for it. Vehicles of all kinds, drawn by horses or mules, clattered through muddy streets strewn with discarded fish bones, rotting vegetables, and rubbish of all kinds. Some streets were nearly blocked with everything from cases of fine wines to barrels of salted oysters and sardines, and bales of tobacco, as there was no room for them in the warehouses.

The buildings were large and looked imposing, but the Argonauts would soon find out that it was all a sham. They had been built of discarded wooden planks and stiff canvas paneling painted to look like wood or stone. The town was obviously given over to wild living. Gambling houses and saloons stood side by side with staid business offices. Everything in the city was extravagantly expensive. As one Argonaut wrote home, "Money here goes like dirt; everything costs a dollar or dollars. What is considered a fortune at home is here mere pocket money. And as if to top it all," he adds, "today I purchased a single potato for forty-five cents."

In this jumble of noise and color the Argonauts began searching out supply houses to make sure they had everything needed for the great adventure. It was then they learned that their crucibles, gold-washing retorts, and gold-testing equipment were worthless. All that was really necessary was a round, flat-bottomed iron pan, a shovel, a pick, and a strong knife.

Those who had invested their money in a ship and cargo to make a great killing learned to their dismay that plenty of ships were already rotting in the bay, and unless the goods in the cargo were in demand, there would be no sale. This meant that

The women gathered in front of the French millinery store represent four of the different nationalities in California in 1849. On the left, a modest Chinese housewife; beside her, a coquettish Mexican señorita and her sober chaperone. On the right, an elegant Southern lady accompanied by her black maid.

San Francisco's rainy season turned the streets into rivers of mud. Women as well as men made knee-high boots a necessary part of their dress.

most of the speculators were left almost penniless. They would have to find employment in San Francisco to earn enough capital even to go to the gold fields.

During the time the Argonauts stayed in San Francisco, they had to find a place to board. That was when they discovered how expensive lodging was. Boardinghouses and the several hotels in town were just as flimsy as everything else. In the cheaper boardinghouses sleeping quarters were narrow bunks set up in a common room. Guests had to bring their own bedding.

In the more expensive hotels like the old St. Francis, tiny individual rooms were separated from one another by paper walls. Ceilings were often made of canvas

The St. Francis Hotel of 1849 boasted individual rooms, though the rooms were narrow and the walls between them were paper. But the blankets and sheets were clean, and the restaurant, though housed in a canvas tent, served gourmet meals.

that rippled and billowed with every gust of wind. The city was a firetrap and frequently whole blocks were swept by flames fanned by wild sea winds. But there was one bright spot—the meals. They might be high priced, but they were usually delicious.

Many of the Argonauts were too strapped for money to even consider staying in a boardinghouse. Instead, they pitched tents on the slopes of the hills that surrounded the bay. But no one stayed there long if he could help it.

As soon as possible the Argonauts left the city. Some traveled by stagecoach, others by steamboat up the Sacramento River to Sutter's Fort and the little town of Sacramento. There they found Sutter and the merchants vying with one another for the trade of those passing through. During their short stay in Sacramento, the Argonauts asked for advice as to the best locations for finding gold.

Depending on the advice they received, they set out for one location or another. Some went alone on horseback, on a mule, or afoot. Others went in a company. Eyes bright with anticipation, they hurried toward the towering Sierra Nevada where gold lay everywhere, or so they imagined.

Telegraph Hill, its slopes dotted with the tents of squatters, overlooks the entrance to San Francisco Bay. The semaphore perched atop its highest point used different colored flags to announce the arrival and origin of each ship as it entered the bay.

Gold

EW IF ANY GOLD SEEKERS WONDERED WHERE THE gold they were after came from. Scientists theorize that it, like other minerals, originated deep within the earth. They suggest it has been brought closer to the earth's surface by volcanic activity that heats large underground water supplies. The boiling water liquifies the gold and then rises, carrying the gold along with it. The water floods the upper layers of rock and then recedes, leaving the hardening gold behind, lodged in the cracks and crevices of the rocks. These golden veins are called lodes. A network of such lodes is called a mother lode. The Mother Lode stretches north to south for several hundred miles of the Sierra Nevada, where gold is found in quartz rock formations.

These gold-bearing rocks have been brought closer to the surface by tectonic drift. According to scientists, the earth's land masses drift slowly over the earth's surface. When they push against each other, they create towering mountains, bringing the rocks upward with them.

Over countless millennia, wind and rain have been eroding the earth above these rocks, exposing the veins of gold. Heavy rains scour the gold out of the veins, and raging torrents carry the bits and pieces away. Gold, a heavy metal, sinks to the bottom of the streams. There the fragments are roiled about by rocks, pebbles, and coarse gravel, creating small nuggets, thin golden flakes, or even gold dust as fine as flour.

Mining equipment used by forty-niners: flat-bottomed pan, cradle, pickax, handheld scales, a miner's lantern, a pouch in which to store gold dust.

When the rains stop and the streams lose their force, the gold is dropped in the stream beds or it is trapped in the cracks and crevices of the ledges that occasionally form along river banks. Sometimes it may lie hidden just beneath the surface soil of river valleys. These deposits of loose gold are known as placer gold. Beginning miners in the Sierra Nevada collected the placer gold by panning. All that was needed for the job was a shovel, a pick, a dipper, and an iron pan with a flat bottom.

The miner selected a likely spot beside a stream and then shoveled dirt into his pan. He used the dipper to pour the water into the pan and swirled it gently round and round. Then he tipped the pan slightly to one side to let the water flow out, carrying away the grit and gravel, while the gold sank to the bottom.

More seasoned miners moved on to a better method of gleaning gold. It was called the cradle or rocker method. A cradle could be bought, or it could be made by anyone with some carpentry skills. It was an open box, three to four feet long, which rested on rockers. A series of cleats, or "ripples," as the miners called them, were fastened to the floor of the cradle. A tall box with an open top—the hopper—was attached to the upper end of the cradle. At its base, the hopper opened onto the floor of the cradle. The entranceway was closed by a coarse sieve that strained out the larger rocks, while letting the finer debris through.

Sometimes a partnership of only two worked the cradle, but this meant fewer periods of rest.

The cradle was placed in a slightly slanted position and was operated by two or three partners. One man would dig up loads of dirt and gravel and drop them into the hopper. The second man would bring water from the stream and pour it onto the dirt and gravel in the hopper. The third man, often a boy, would operate the rockers by pushing and pulling a long handle attached to them. The gentle movement of the rockers had the same effect as panning: It kept the gravel, silt, and sand moving gently out of the cradle while the heavier gold was left behind, trapped by the ripples.

Working with a cradle was not as backbreaking as panning. It also gave the men a chance to exchange jobs so they wouldn't have to do the same thing over and over all day long. But the cradle proved not to be as efficient as the miners had wished. When they realized how much gold the short cradle was losing, they sometimes exchanged it for another implement—the Long Tom, which was just a longer version of the cradle. Because it was larger and heavier than the cradle, it also required several men to operate it.

The Long Tom was twelve or more feet long, eight to eighteen inches wide, and some inches high. Its floor, like that of the cradle, was broken up by a series of ripples. A sieve enclosed the opening at the head of the Long Tom, which was laid at a slant in the bed of a fast-running stream.

If the gold happened to be at a distance from the stream, the men would dig a ditch to connect the two and lay the Long Tom in that. The flow of water through the Long Tom would take the place of panning or rocking. The men took turns at the work. Some shoveled dirt and gravel into the Long Tom. Others spaced themselves along its length and gently stirred the gravel with

The Long Tom, much heavier than the cradle, required more operators. But they were repaid with greater harvests of gold than the shorter cradle produced.

their shovels to keep it moving along to the end, where it would be carried off, leaving the gold behind, trapped by the ripples.

The Long Tom acted like a sluice, that is a channel through which water runs flushing out debris. Sometimes the Long Tom was lengthened with a series of smaller sluice boxes. These were also equipped with ripples and attached, one after the other, to the end of the Long Tom so that the water would flow through them too.

In gold-rich areas the miners were sometimes able to create natural sluices.

By diverting a stream so that the water flows over a shallow ledge, these miners have created a natural sluice. At the top of the miniature fall they shovel in loads of gold-bearing debris, and retrieve the gold from the shallow pool at its base.

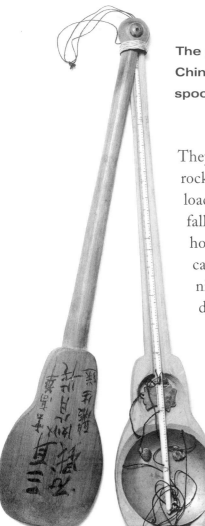

The pocket scales for measuring gold dust were used by Chinese miners, as the Chinese characters written on the spoon reveal.

They diverted a nearby stream into a ditch leading to a low ledge of rock, creating a miniature waterfall. The men then began shoveling loads of gold-bearing debris into the water at the head of the little fall. The debris was carried down to a shallow basin the men had hollowed out at the base of the ledge. While the lighter debris was carried off the heavier gold sank and could be retrieved by panning. All these methods of collecting placer gold were called "wet diggings."

"Dry Diggings" were done when the site was too far away from water to make use of it. Then the gold would be separated from the dry earth by winnowing. Old-time farmers used to winnow their grain by placing it in a big tray and tossing it gently up and down to get rid of chaff and dust, leaving the heavier grain behind. Unfortunately winnowing wasn't of much use to the miners, because the fine gold dust would blow away, too.

However hard a prospector might work searching for gold, seasoned miners claimed that in the end everything depended on luck, and Luck is a fickle lady. She laughs at the solemn pronouncements of geologists, most of whom left the gold fields empty-handed. Instead Luck often smiles on the most ignorant of men. Just by chance, someone might kick away a stone on which he had stubbed his toe to find the glint of golden treasure below. Or he might follow a rabbit to its gold-speckled hole, or a wandering cow to a hill, where he would discover exposed rocks laced with gold—or so ran the stories miners told around their campfires at night.

The Diggings

THE ARGONAUTS MUST HAVE FOUND THEMSELVES in a strange world once they left the valley behind and entered the foothills of the Sierra Nevada. In tier after tier the towering peaks rose before them. Underfoot noisy streams rushed through steep beds on their way to the valley. Forests of pine and cedar clothed the slopes—the home of grizzlies, mountain lions, lively squirrels, and gentle deer. Nights were given over to the howling of wolves, the yapping of coyotes, the haunting calls of owls. It was a place of mystery, of fear, the place of the miners' diggings.

Most of the diggings were along the banks of the rivers and streams, which were lined here and there by knots of prospectors working almost silently, some standing knee-deep in the icy water. Not noticing the grandeur of the world around them, they were intent only on one thing—the glimmer of gold that told them they had hit pay dirt.

The Argonaut entering this bewildering world was fortunate if he could call on the advice of a seasoned prospector about the best way to select a promising spot and claim it. This was a painstaking process. It consisted of digging with a shovel to discover what lay under the thin layer of soil deposited by some recent freshet, or using a pick or knife to dig into a ridge to see if there was any hidden gold in it.

Once the new gold seeker had chosen his spot, he would have to spend time

In the rugged foothills of the Sierra Nevada groups of miners like these were so occupied with their solitary task that they had no eye for the grandeur around them.

watching and trying to copy the tricky skills of panning. It had to be done with a lot of gentle movements, or the gold would slip out with the gravel. Panning was especially hard on the back because the panner would have to hold the pan while in a half-bent position. To make matters even worse, he might have to stand in a stream of icy water to do the job.

The search for gold went on from first dawn to dusk. Only when the gleam of gold

no longer shone out in the deepen-
ing twilight would the miners drop
their work and head for their camp-
ground. The camp was just a jumble
of tents and shanties crowded together,
and there wasn't much room inside
any of them. But room wasn't needed.
Besides their mining tools, the miners
had few possessions. These usually
consisted of one change of under-
garments, a red flannel shirt and
a gray flannel shirt, two pairs of
woolen pants, and one or two blankets. Sleeping arrangements were
simple. A miner wrapped himself in
one or both blankets and slept on the
bare ground, no matter how soggy it
might be from recent rains.

Cooking and eating utensils were
few—a skillet and spatula, a coffee
pot and cup, a plate and a spoon and
fork. Perhaps if the miner had a little
money he might also own a Dutch

The eyes of all three men are
glued on the water slipping through
one man's fingers, hoping for the
glimmer that will tell them they
have struck gold.

oven. Usually the miner did his cooking over an open fire outside his tent, but if he
had a wooden shack, he might have an open fireplace or a crude stove of some kind
inside. His meals consisted of hardtack mixed with water and boiled with bacon,
ham, or salt pork to make a porridge. But often the porridge was full of weevils,
unnoticed by the miner in the dim light.

Six days a week the miners kept at their backbreaking work. Sundays were set
aside as their day of leisure. What they did on this day is recorded in the numerous
diaries the miners filled. They wrote that Sunday was the day for laundering, of
necessity done by men in those early all-male camps. It was a job most of them
thoroughly hated. Still, it had to be done, and all over camp on Sundays was heard

Sunday at the diggings.

the sound of vigorous scrubbing. Some of the men, though, took a shortcut by simply soaking their dirty clothes in water, then hanging them on a clothesline to be rinsed again and again by rains and pummeled by recurrent blasts of wind until finally they were ready to be worn again.

The miners paid little attention to their hair or mustaches and beards. All grew long and tangled and went unwashed like the clothes. And both harbored hordes of lice and fleas. Sundays were also set aside for going through the seams of their clothes and tangles of hair to shake out the lice that had taken up living quarters there.

Some men spent the rest of their spare time whittling. Others read books or wrote home or brought their diaries up to date. If there was a fiddler in camp, or someone with a good singing voice, he might be asked to give an impromptu musical performance. At such times the miners would be sure to burst into one of their favorite songs, sung to the tune of "O Susanna." It rang out into the night, deep throated and boisterous:

O, Susanna, O don't you cry for me,
I'm off to Californi-ay with my washbowl on my knee...

Sometimes Sunday amusements were put together at a moment's notice—a horse race, a footrace, a dogfight. But much of the miners' spare time was spent spinning tall tales.

Days scheduled for the arrival of mail and supplies were always red-letter days to the camp, as by that time food supplies were dwindling. The miners clustered around the wagons, from which supplies were sold directly. Temporary scales were devised and values in gold dust were set. Food supplies consisted of quantities of ship's hardtack, salted pork, bacon, and ham, as well as dried beans for the Mexican miners and rice for the Chinese.

Rarely there might be dried apples and peaches, or perhaps some kegs of preserved oysters, luxuries to be used on very special occasions. Meat was never sold by the wagon suppliers, but by hunters in from the forests with a deer or rabbits, or by ranch hands with a cow for sale. Meat was a rare and wonderful treat. But there was always an abundance of whiskey.

The poor diet and the constant exposure to cold and rain resulted in illnesses—rheumatism, fevers, chills, dysentery, diarrhea, tuberculosis. There were also epidemics of cholera and typhoid. Many suffered from scurvy because they lacked fruits and vegetables in their diet. Usually the miners treated their illnesses with the medicinal cures they had brought along—chamomile tea, quinine, laudanum, opium preparation, and various other kinds of household remedies.

Along with illness there was the constant threat of food poisoning, especially from the oysters. And then there were accidents, many of them serious. Deaths were not infrequent and were followed by funerals conducted with simple rites. The corpse was wrapped in a blanket or placed in a crude wooden coffin and buried in an unmarked grave. Another dreamer who had left home with such high hopes would never return to it again.

At these times death, and the darkness of impending death, cast a gloomy cloud of loss and intense homesickness upon those left behind. Many Argonauts just gave up and drifted back to Sacramento and San Francisco to take up any kind of employment open to them. All they wanted now was to earn enough money for the passage home. Those in the professional fields—doctors, teachers, accountants— found employment easily. The others took whatever jobs were available—porters to handle the goods brought by incoming ships, waiters in restaurants, clerks in shops, hospital orderlies, boardinghouse workers. They enriched the city's expanding services.

chapter 8

Large Settlements

THE ARGONAUTS WHO LEFT THE GOLD FIELDS weren't missed. Their places were taken by hordes of others drawn by the lure of gold. Some eighty thousand strong, they swarmed over the foothills of the Sierra Nevada.

Among them were adventurers, the educated, the illiterate, con men, criminals, drifters. They came from all parts of the world, from South as well as North America, the British Isles, France, Germany, Australia, China, Malaysia, the Hawaiian Islands, Mexico. There were also some Native Americans who had by this time learned the value of the white man's gold.

The first newcomers began to work the easily reached places. But when, lined shoulder to shoulder, they had exhausted gold along the banks of the

Miners set off for a new location rumored to be rich in placer gold.

If gold was found in any quantity, a small camp quickly grew. Among the first accommodations appearing in such camps was a boardinghouse. Often it was little more than a tent to shelter men from the rain and provide both food and whiskey.

most accessible rivers and streams, they began to move out into more remote locations. The rumor of a newly found gold strike caused groups of miners to desert their digs and rush off for a look at the new strike.

If it proved to be a genuine find, they settled there to work a claim. A new mining camp was formed. As it grew in size, the miners spread out to discover fresh strikes in the vicinity. Other smaller camps sprang up at these sites, and the large camp served as a hub for the smaller ones.

As a hub grew in size, San Francisco traders saw the value of establishing general stores there. They stocked the shelves with all kinds of salable merchandise—everything from food and drink to mining equipment, blankets, and kitchenware. Often the mining camps were in such isolated areas, and the trails to them so hazardous, that wagons couldn't be used for transport. Trains of pack mules were used instead. There might be as many as 150 mules in the train.

There was one stretch of the trail to the mountain town of Downieville that was so narrow travelers could not pass each other on it, let alone pack mules. One chronicler describes how the mules had been trained to handle the problem:

"Those loaded with cargo kept steadily up the trail, while empty mules scrambled up the steep bank, where they stood still until the others had passed. It not infrequently happened, however, that a loaded mule got crowded off the trail . . ." There is no record of how many mules lost their lives on that dangerous passage.

Carting supplies to such remote places meant higher prices for the customers. Cheating shopkeepers also added to the expense. Occasionally the miners complained, but so long as they had an easy supply of gold, they didn't really mind. After all, they were eager to change their fare of hardtack and salt pork for tins of sardines and oysters, pickled tongue, even turtle soup and lobster salad in tins.

Muleteers driving teams of mules stop at the hotel and headquarters of this mining town to unload huge wagons piled high with various goods. They will supply not only the large hub camp but also all its surrounding satellite camps.

There was also an almost inexhaustible supply of whiskey, and even champagne. An ounce of gold was estimated to be worth ten dollars. It would buy a bottle of champagne or a pound of gunpowder or a chicken.

Often the general store served as the town saloon, and the counter was also the bar. Behind it, whiskey bottles sat side by side with canned fish, bottled pickles, and tins of sardines. Business was informal. On snowy days when the miners couldn't work, they gathered in the general store. Sitting around the table with the shopkeeper, they might spend the day playing the card game seven-up, the loser paying off his bets with drinks all around, bought from the shopkeeper.

The amount of whiskey being sold and the amount of gambling being done caught the attention of saloon and gambling entrepreneurs. Soon the general stores were joined by separate saloons and gambling halls. Some were ornately furnished with chandeliers and large portraits of nude women. These furnishings, too, were carried over the trail by pack mules—no mean feat.

The saloons and gambling halls were followed by cheap hotels, which provided sleeping spaces on the bare floor of a dormitory. There might be a bar in the lobby, and perhaps a dining tent where meals were served.

Most of the mining settlements were still without women. A few did appear there, however, but they went by the unflattering designation of "painted women" or "fallen women." Brothels opened in some of the mining camps. In others they were frowned upon. Sometimes they were even driven out of town.

Husbands felt uneasy about bringing their wives to these rowdy all-male camps, many of which might appear quite homey from a distance. For instance, a visitor looking down into the canyon where Downieville nestled would view a scene as idyllic as a child's toy village. Up close it had a very different look. Housecleaning by the men consisted of throwing all discarded objects out of their houses into the muddy lane that ran past the door. Embedded in the mud were empty sardine tins, worn-out pots and kettles, ragged boots and shirts, old ham bones, broken picks and shovels. Sometimes the lane might also be blocked by zealous miners who were digging it up because it was rumored that someone had found a nugget of gold under the muddy debris.

Though the thought of finding gold filled the miners' lives, many no longer seemed concerned with making a pile of money and then going home with it. Caught

On rainy days and Sundays idle miners liked to gather in the local bar. They would sit around the potbellied stove to gossip, and sometimes there would also be card games and gambling.

As the camp grew, a large township, like this one at Markleeville, was formed with houses, saloons, gambling halls, a general store, and a hotel.

up in the lure of the search, they often didn't prize the treasure, even when it fell into their hands. It was just easy come, easy go. And they might spend a whole day's accumulation of gold dust in a riotous night of gambling and drinking.

Drinking often ended in fistfights over some senseless argument. This might be followed by a huge brawl. Knives might flash. Pistols might be fired. Finally all the saloon customers would pour into the street, some still firing, others trying to escape the flying bullets. Innocent passersby caught in the crossfire were in danger of becoming casualties themselves. On holidays and weekends sensible people quickly retreated outdoors.

In the words of a citizen in Weaverville, one of the wildest of the mining settlements, "Saturday night is usually celebrated by such hideous yells and occasionally a volley from their revolvers, which makes it rather dangerous to be standing around . . . There have been some awfully close shaves. One man has been shot through the cravat, one through the hat, and one in the arm. The Weaverville hotel [a flimsy edifice of lumber and cloth] has been sacked and fistfights without number have come off. But as nobody has been killed, nothing has been done."

chapter 9

Law and Order

AR FROM THE COASTAL AREAS STILL UNDER A loose kind of military rule, the mining towns were free to handle their own crimes and make their own laws and regulations. One of their main concerns was establishing miners' claims. The general rule was to decide the size of a claim by the amount of land the miner could work by himself. He was not allowed to stake out a claim and then sublet it or hold on to it for sale at a higher price. He was not permitted to bring in slaves to do the job for him. To keep his claim he had to spend at least one day a week working it. Usually each camp elected a claims officer. His job was to keep a record of the claims, collecting a small fee for every one he registered.

As the camps grew in size, the number of other crimes, including theft and murder, increased. The miners carried out their own kind of justice to handle these cases. They followed the trappings of court procedure by selecting a jury of twelve or six, or even just three. But they did it on the spot and by mob choice. The juries almost always agreed with the sentence the mob was demanding. And the thoroughly roused mob usually called for a lynching.

The first hanging on the gold fields was in the little town of Dry Diggings, some twenty miles from Coloma. Dry Diggings was already a major transportation center on the trail that led over the Sierra Nevada into California. By 1849, tents had given way to log cabins or board-and-shingle houses. The town's saloons were flourishing, and its gambling halls attracted professional gamblers. In the winter of 1849 one of these gamblers, after winning big at poker, retired to his room for the night. There he was surprised by five men, one of whom held a pistol to his head while the others went through his belongings, searching for his winnings. When they found his stack of gold, they pocketed it, released the gambler, and fled.

Judge Brown held trials in a carpenter's shop at one mining town.

The thieves were caught almost at once. Two hundred miners gathered to pass judgment. The verdict was thirty-five lashes on the bare back. This done, the men were released. But when the miners learned that the three were also wanted for robbery and attempted murder on the Stanislaus River, they quickly passed another sentence—death to all three. Only one man dared speak out against this summary decision. But he was drowned out by the persistent bellows of the crowd, "Hang them! Hang them!"

Action followed. Three ropes ending in nooses were hung from the limbs of a nearby tree. Then the men were forced to climb onto the bed of a wagon hitched to a horse. The horse was led forward until the wagon was under the limbs where the three ropes hung. The nooses were placed around the necks of the men. Then the sharp flick of a whip sent the horses dashing forward, leaving the three men dangling in midair—a warning to all who came that way: Crime will be harshly dealt with here.

From then on the town of Dry Diggings was called Hangtown. And hanging became the normal procedure for other gold towns, too. There must have been a lot of them, for in the words of one contemporary traveler, "The oaks were tasseled with the carcasses of the wicked."

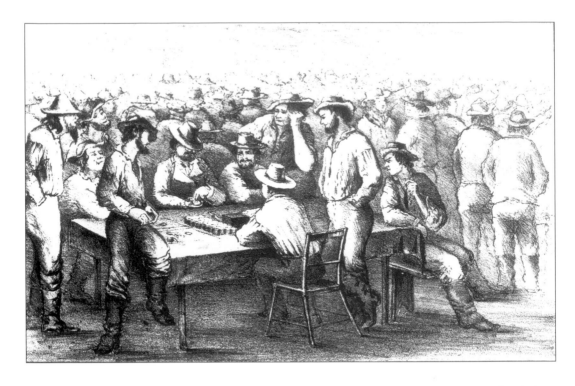

On Saturday nights, Sundays, and all holidays the gambling halls of mining towns were crowded with drinking, card-playing miners.

Despite the near reverence most miners showed toward women, they still hanged one July 5, 1851. Her name was Juanita, a beautiful Mexican national who lived with her Mexican lover in a small cabin outside the mining town of Downieville. After a two-day holiday drinking binge, a miner broke down Juanita's door in what he claimed was an accident, and stumbled inside. He returned the next day, having sobered, to make his apologies to Juanita. But in the course of that apology he insulted her with such degrading epithets, according to her story, that in a moment of passion the fiery Juanita picked up a knife and fatally stabbed him.

Immediately the miners convened court. Despite the pleas of two men, the miners immediately and in one loud voice pronounced Juanita guilty and sentenced her to death by hanging.

Juanita was escorted to a hastily constructed scaffold. She walked to it with her head held high. In dignified silence she mounted the barrel placed there for her and pulled back her long, thick braids to adjust the noose around her neck. Then with a final wave and a pleasant "Adios, amigos," she stepped calmly off into space.

Watching her die, the miners suddenly sobered. They left quietly, ashamed of what they had done—hanged a woman for defending her honor. The stigma of that hanging was to cling to Downieville for years to come.

Juanita, the beautiful Mexican señorita, victim of one of the holiday brawls, delivers her brave adieu from the gallows.

Statehood

EIGHTEEN FORTY-NINE WAS A YEAR OF DECISION for the province of California. When it was ceded to the United States on May 2, 1848, it was a sleepy place with only ten thousand inhabitants, mostly Hispanic and Native American. Mexico had always considered the province a rather unproductive tract of land, given over mostly to large ranches. The people who lived there didn't need much regulation. For the most part, they followed old ways and customs.

When President Polk named Colonel Mason governor of California, Mason followed the Mexican laws and customs. This worked well enough until the discovery of gold in the foothills of the Sierra Nevada and the explosion of immigrants that followed. By 1849 the population had reached some one hundred thousand people, and it was still growing. The formerly quiet pastoral and agricultural province was now a bustling maelstrom of newcomers, many with shady pasts. Old laws and customs could not control the rising crime rate in cities as well as in isolated mining communities. Vigilante practices were becoming common everywhere.

California needed a suitable set of laws. But no one there had the authority to set up a legislature that could make the laws. That authority had to come from the United States Congress, which was also required to provide guidelines for the governing body.

The first step was to apply for statehood. Governor Mason was asked to forward

Among the representatives who gathered to write the state constitution in Monterey were men like these miners. They stored their tools and left their diggings even even if it might mean risking having someone steal their claims. They felt it their civic duty, even if they only went as spectators.

an application and did so at once. It was expected that California would be accepted immediately. It had a large population and more wealth at its disposal than any state already in the Union.

But instead of the expected rapid response, the months passed without any word from Washington. The problem was that California had applied as a free state at a time when North and South were locked in a bitter struggle—free states against slave states. At the time California applied, the Senate was evenly divided: fifteen members from the North, fifteen members from the South. If California was admitted, the number of senators from the North would increase to sixteen, upsetting the balance of power. The South was not about to let that happen. So they wrangled on.

Living without any kind of legitimate government was becoming intolerable to the Californians. More and more people were demanding that they hold their own convention, write their own constitution, and elect their own legislative body. Newspapers took up the cry.

Finally a delegation appealed to Governor Mason to sanction a convention, but he refused, claiming he had no authority to do so. Things were at an impasse until General Bennett Riley succeeded Mason as governor. Acting on his own, Riley called for a constitutional convention to be held in Monterey. But his proclamation raised doubts in many people, who felt that the call should have come from a civilian rather than a military man.

The problem was resolved when a civilian named Peter H. Burnett took charge. He arranged for a committee of citizens to call for another convention to start at the same time and in the same place as Riley's. Thus two conventions held jointly in the same hall would provide a double sanction for the operation, even though neither had any legitimate claim to do so.

Once the date of the conventions was set, agents traveled throughout the territory, calling for delegates to design a fitting state constitution. On August 1, 1849, an election for delegates was held. The delegates met September 1, 1849. The meeting was presided over by Dr. Robert Semple, a newspaper editor.

Forty-eight delegates responded to the roll call. Among them were seven Hispanic Californians and one delegate each from Ireland, Scotland, Spain, France, and Switzerland. The rest were Americans. Twenty-two had lived in California for three years or more. Twenty-four were lawyers. Twelve were farmers. Seven were merchants. Others were engineers, doctors, bankers, and printers. There were also a number of representatives from the mining communities, who had given up their digs to attend the convention. Since most of them knew little about law, they were there mostly as spectators.

Work on the new constitution was slow and painstaking. The constitutions of other states were studied carefully, and the most useful items in them were extracted and adapted. The document was finally completed and signed by the delegates on October 13, 1849.

Cannons boomed to announce the historic event. Flags flew from every business house in Monterey. Copies of the constitution, along with ballots listing the names of the nominees for the state assembly and the state senator, were distributed by the thousands. One month after its completion, the constitution was ratified by a majority of fifteen to one, and the nominees for the various offices were chosen. Only one sixth of the population had voted, but among that sixth the miners had done their part.

Many miners were voting for the first time in their lives, and they were excited at the prospect. Though they didn't bother to read the constitution, they readily voted to ratify it. As for the candidates on the ballot, few if any of the miners knew who they were, but they made their choices all the same. One candidate whose last name was Fair received a good number of votes. The voters liked his name, which seemed to indicate a fair man. Another nominee lost thirty votes because someone had seen him on a Sacramento riverboat, wearing a stovepipe hat, a sure sign of snobbery.

Perhaps the reasoning of most is best expressed by the words of one of the voters: "When I left home I was determined to go it blind. I went it blind in coming to California and I'm not going to stop now. I voted for the constitution and I've never seen the constitution. I voted for all the candidates and I don't know a damned one of them. I'm going it blind all through, I am."

A typical mining camp polling place was described by an observer who was present at the tent city of Mokelumne Hill on voting day. According to him the day was rainy,

Sacramento was named the state capital in 1954.

cold and clammy, November weather. Few people cared to venture out until noon, when the inspectors arrived. They set up polling booths in the saloon, which was housed in the largest tent in town. According to the observer, "The inspectors took their seats behind the counter in close proximity to the glasses and bottles, the calls for which were quite as frequent as the votes."

On December 15, 1848, newly elected Governor Burnett called the new legislature together. It was realized then that no city had been chosen to be the capital of the state. For several years the capital would be a floating one, moving from city to city until 1954, when Sacramento was finally chosen.

The first legislature met in San Jose. Among the items on the legislature's agenda was the election of two United States senators, in readiness for the day California would achieve statehood. One of the men elected for the position was Colonel John C. Frémont. Frémont was a controversial figure, idolized by many

The bear on the flag raised by John C. Frémont and his followers actually looked more like a pig.

Californians, criticized as harshly by others. He was an officer in the United States Army, as well as an explorer for the national government.

In 1846 he had led a small company of settlers and trappers in a revolt against the Mexican government, after hearing rumors that it planned to expel them from California. They marched under a flag which featured a grizzly striding across a white background that also contained the Lone Star emblem of Texas, which was fighting for independence from Mexico too. (Derisive Mexicans said that the drawing looked more like a pig than a bear.)

The Bear Flag Army marched into Sonoma on June 14, and without any bloodshed, captured the nonresisting general, Mariano

When the voting for United States senator took place, John C. Frémont was elected on the first ballot.

Guadalupe Vallejo, the ranking Mexican army officer there. The rebels raised their flag and proclaimed California a new republic. The new republic lasted one month. On July 7, regular United States forces marched into Monterey, the capital. They lowered the Mexican flag and raised the United States' Stars and Stripes. But the Bear Flag was not to be forgotten. In later years, with a more accurately drawn bear, it was chosen California's state flag.

Following the end of the war with Mexico, Frémont applied for the governorship of California. He was opposed by Brigadier General Stephen Watts Kearny, who was then in charge of the California forces, of which Frémont was a member. The quarrel over this issue became so heated between the two men that Kearny accused Frémont of insubordination and sent him to Washington for a court-martial.

Frémont was acquitted, and resigned from the California army unit in anger. He returned to the state an even greater hero and immediately ran for the United States Senate. To no one's surprise, he was elected on the first ballot. It took a third ballot to elect the other senator, William Gwin, a Southern sympathizer who had managed to keep the depth of his allegiance to the South concealed.

Celebrations like this one in San Francisco on the fourth of July, 1851 were held all over California when the word came that statehood had finally been granted.

Now there was a problem. One of the two senators would have only a few months in office, since that term would expire when the new Senate convened in January. The other elected senator would serve the usual six-year term. It was decided to draw lots. Gwin won the longer term.

Meanwhile the Senate in Washington, D.C. was finally able to solve its dilemma with the involved Compromise of 1850. At last senators were free to vote on California's application for statehood. On September 9, 1850, President Millard Fillmore signed the bill that formally admitted California into the Union. The news reached California on October 15 and was greeted by cheering crowds in cities across the state. Newspapers covering the story were snapped up at the exorbitant price of five dollars apiece.

Nowhere was the news received with greater acclaim than in mining country. Swept by a wave of patriotism, the miners celebrated with parades and ceremonies featuring long-winded speakers. Everyone drank toasts to the new state in saloons and hotel bars.

The celebrations spilled out into the muddy streets of gold towns, to the roars of excited miners. Pistols popped, shotguns blasted. The revelry continued until the last available bottle of whiskey had been downed. Only then did men begin to remember that they would go hungry unless they got back to their diggings.

chapter 11

The Mother Lode Discovered

FRÉMONT HAD PLENTY TO OCCUPY HIS TIME in California. In 1847 he had sent three thousand dollars to the American consul in Monterey, asking him to purchase a ranch for him outside the city of San Jose. Instead the consul bought forty-five thousand acres of what Frémont soon discovered was worthless real estate. Despite Frémont's bitter complaints the consul refused to take back the land and return Frémont's three thousand dollars. He was stuck with a worthless ranch that went by the Spanish name of Mariposa, or "butterfly."

For two years Frémont seethed with resentment. But in 1849 his fortunes changed. His supposedly worthless ranch was discovered to contain rich placer gold deposits. The news brought forty-niners scurrying to the site. Ignoring Frémont's right to the land, they began jumping claims. Claim jumping was a favorite sport on the mining fields, and making it easier for the claim jumpers on Frémont's land, his deed showed no precise boundaries.

So many claim jumpers arrived that they founded a town, Mariposa, on a piece of Frémont's property. The new town wasn't a tranquil place. The inhabitants kept fighting with one another over creek beds and gold-rich embankments. Periodically Frémont cleared the town of the squatters only to have more rush in to take their place.

Then in August of the same year, an important discovery was made in beautiful

John C. Frémont's mining operations were located in this idyllic setting. The dam he built on the Merced River provided water in quantity for his mining operations.

Bear Valley, part of Frémont's Mariposa holdings. Rich veins of gold were uncovered in a solid quartz ledge. The farther down one dug, the more gold-veined quartz was found. At last, a section of the great mother lode had been discovered.

   To get at it, Frémont would have to sink deep mines. Eventually he would have three of them—the Black Drift, the Josephine, and the Pine Tree. Unfortunately the story of the big discovery spread and began bringing in a new kind of claim jumper. They were organized groups of miners who weren't after the placer gold. They were interested in mining the mother lode. The most aggressive was the Merced Mining Company. Claiming that Frémont's mines lay beyond the

The cottage where Jessie Frémont spent so many pleasant days until the threats of the Merced miners destroyed her peace.

boundaries of his land deed, they took over two of them—the Black Drift and the Josephine.

Their attack came at a critical time for Frémont. It was 1856, a presidential election year, and the Republican Party had named John Frémont their nominee. Campaigning took up Frémont's time until election day. He lost to James Buchanan and early in 1857 returned to California, where he immediately filed suit to reclaim his lost mines.

But the danger wasn't over. The Merced owners were now after his Pine Tree mine, and Frémont had to be constantly on guard against them. Still, he felt secure enough by the summer of 1858 to bring his wife, Jessie, and their three children to live with him in the little bungalow he had built near the Pine Tree.

Frémont was soon to be tested. One dark night fifty Merced miners set out to take over the Pine Tree by stealth. Frémont learned of the plot and posted six well-armed men at the mouth of the mine. The men threw up a breastwork of huge boulders, mining equipment, and barrels of gunpowder. When they heard the Merced men at the entrance to the tunnel, they shouted a threat.

"Come a step into the tunnel and we'll blow it up! We won't let you take the mine!"

The Merced men were stopped. But they still had other moves. They posted guards around the mouth of the tunnel to keep the men inside from getting supplies of food, hoping this would starve them out. Tit for tat! Frémont surrounded the Merced men with a ring of his own, preventing them from getting supplies, too.

The local sheriff came out to settle the dispute by ordering the Merced men off Frémont's property. They ignored him. The sheriff was too understaffed to carry any clout.

Frémont realized that if he wanted real help, he would have to appeal to the governor of the state. The governor alone had the power to dispatch the state militia to bring order to Mariposa. Frémont sent out a messenger to inform the governor of the problem, only to have the man intercepted and sent back by a Merced guard. Frémont sent messenger after messenger, with the same result. He discovered then that the Merced people had posted guards at every trail leading out of the Mariposa ranch.

The situation looked desperate until a daring young Englishman named Douglas Fox, who was then visiting at the Frémont home, decided to take on the challenge himself. Mounting his horse, he set off secretly. Not choosing a trail, but sticking to the thick brush, he threaded his way across the Mariposa lands and slipped through the trap the Merced guards had set.

Once free of the ranch, young Fox galloped off for Coulterville, the nearest town. From Coulterville, relays of riders carrying Frémont's request raced through the wide San Joaquin River valley to the city of Stockton. There the last rider rushed to the local telegraph office and sent Frémont's urgent message by wire to the governor at Sacramento.

Meanwhile, the Merced group was getting more and more threatening. One day when Frémont was absent from the cottage, his wife, Jessie, got a furtive visitor who handed her a horrifying note. In twenty-four hours, it read, the cottage would be burned to the ground. Leave at once!

Jessie stared at the note, considering

The entrance to the Pine Tree mine in Bear Valley. Frémont's men were ready to blast the entrance shut to keep out the Merced miners.

Jessie Frémont as a young woman.

what to do. She knew that Fox had escaped the Merced trap, because he hadn't come back. The question now was: Had he been able to get word to the governor? And would the governor respond in time? She came to a quick decision and began writing a note, which she asked the messenger to take back to the Merced men. The note explained that there was no need to endanger her family's life to make them leave. She only asked for a little more time, so that she could pack some family belongings.

The man took the note and left. Jessie watched him go, hoping her stall would work, because all she was really bargaining for was just a little more time for the governor to reply. But Jessie couldn't be sure the Merced men would honor her plea, and as the hours went by she had to keep fighting off her panic.

There's no telling what might have happened if an official messenger hadn't come riding pell-mell to the Pine Tree mine to deliver the governor's order to the Merced miners. It was short and stern: Leave the Mariposa, or the state militia will be dispatched against you.

The Merced men left at once. They were no longer a threat to the Frémonts. Jessie and her children could again ride horseback through the lovely wilderness areas of Mariposa where on a clear day they could see the rocky entrance to beautiful Yosemite Valley from the top of one of the trails. Jessie and her husband could again enjoy evenings entertaining such famous guests as the journalist Horace Greeley and the seafaring writer Richard Henry Dana. But for Jessie the magic she had once felt at the Mariposa ranch was gone. She could no longer enjoy the rides or feel at peace in the cheerful little cottage.

In the spring of 1859, Frémont bought his wife a house in San Francisco and soon joined her there. By this time he had won his lawsuit, but it was a bitter victory. In 1861, saddled with debt, he lost control of Mariposa, to which he never returned. Like Sutter, he had seemed to hold untold wealth in his hands, only to see it slip away. Luck was indeed a fickle lady!

Grass Valley Bonanza

S PLACER GOLD BECAME SCARCE ON THE SURFACE of the earth, miners began looking elsewhere for it. They had discovered that the gold was usually found mixed with gravel and sand that had been trapped in rocky ledges or in pockets of rocks in streambeds. Miners now began digging into the earth of hillsides, looking for underground jumbles of rock that might hold trapped gold. The hills of towns like little Nevada City became pockmarked with these holes, which came to be called "coyote holes" because they looked like the dens coyotes dig for themselves.

Some miners dug shallow holes—a foot or two deep at most. Others went farther and farther down in their search for a bed of rocks, which often indicated an ancient river bed. The deeper tunnels needed to be worked by partners. Once one of the partners came to jumbles of rock, he would begin digging short side tunnels in search of pockets of dirt and gravel. When he found them, he would fill his bucket with the debris and signal to his partner, probably with a jerk on the rope. His partner, waiting above, would haul the bucket up and start panning its contents for gold.

When the tunnels the miners dug were as deep as a hundred feet, they would set up a windlass to get the dirt out. A windlass is a simple device consisting of a roller suspended over the mouth of the hole between two upright posts. A rope is wound around the roller, which can be turned with a handle. A bucket tied to the end of the rope can be sent down and drawn up simply by turning the handle. But a hole deep enough to need a windlass was often dangerous because few miners took the trouble to reinforce the tunnels with timber. The man working in the tunnel was always at risk of being crushed to death under the weight of collapsing dirt.

Big mining companies noticed the success of the coyote hole miners and settled on a more efficient way of getting at the hidden treasure. Instead of digging coyote holes, the companies brought huge moveable fire hoses equipped with powerful nozzles to the foothills of the Sierra Nevada. These machines were called monitors.

With the nozzle turned on full force, a stream of water shot out, scrubbing away the topsoil to expose the gold trapped below by the rocks. The water gashed the

Different methods of mining are shown in this picture: In the left foreground a man pans for gold. In the left background a man sits by his cradle. In the right-hand foreground men are working the Long Tom. In the center men are using a windlass to lower a bucket into a coyote hole. The entrances in the hillside show the presence of a deep mine.

The all-out attack on the Sierra Nevada foothills by hydraulic mining required so much water that it robbed the agricultural valley below of irrigation water.

slopes of the mountains with deep, barren canyons. It left ugly, jagged cliffs scoured clean of soil and vegetation of all kinds.

This sort of mining was called hydraulic mining. Large quantities of water were needed for the operation, and the hydraulic mining companies dug deep canals so they could bring water to a site. Sometimes the canals ran for miles. Some rivers and streams were dammed to create deep reservoirs for the operation, cutting off water in many rivers and streams needed for irrigation by the farmers in the valley below. Instead, the scouring waters spilled dirt, gravel, and debris over the fields and into the streets of towns.

Sometimes rivers were dammed to provide reservoirs like this one in Coloma.

Meanwhile, people were still looking frantically for other places where the mother lode might be found. Yet the person who found a mother lode deposit even greater than that at the Mariposa did so just by chance. It happened at Grass Valley, which lies much farther north than the Mariposa and is near the Yuba River.

The story of how it was found is one of those magical fairy tales that turns out to be true. George Knight, a miner, was following his wandering cow to a low hill covered with pines. At the foot of the hill Knight stubbed his toe. Looking down, he saw that he had unearthed a quartz rock. He picked it up and examined it. A glitter caught his eye. Rushing back to his cabin with the rock, he pounded it into fragments and swirled the gravelly pieces around in his pan. He saw at the bottom a rich golden carpet—*Eureka!* The mother lode discovered!

Like Sutter, like Frémont, like all the other delighted discoverers of gold, Knight could not keep his secret. *Gold! Gold! Gold! The mother lode herself!* The news spread

Overhead flumes, canals, and ditches carried water to extensive mining operations, like this one at Parks' Bar, sometimes extending for miles. By 1855 estimates were that some four hundred miles of waterways had been created in mother lode country.

far and wide—north, south, east, west. There was a run of miners on every supply store in the mining towns, in Sacramento, in San Francisco. Miners by the dozens were purchasing hammers, anvils, mortars, pestles, and every other tool that would serve as a rock crusher.

They bought until the stores everywhere were depleted. Then in a body they descended on Grass Valley—only to find that their efforts wouldn't be enough to tackle the fortress of rock that enclosed the gold.

The Mexicans came next with the contraptions they had been using for years to extract gold from quartz. They were called *arrastras,* and the Mexicans built them on the spot. All it took was a large round bowl or tank which was filled with gold-veined quartz rocks and placed in the center of a circle traced in the earth. A stout wooden pole was anchored in the bowl or tank. And a long wooden arm, or boom, was fastened to the top of the pole. A number of rough heavy millstones were attached by ropes to the arm. When everything was in place a mule with blinders on was tied to the loose end of the arm from which the millstones dangled. As the mule walked round and round the circle the millstones smashed the raw quartz rocks in the bowl or tank, breaking them into bits.

It wasn't long before the *arrastras* were followed by more up-to-date machinery, manufactured by large mining companies formed by investors from businesses and banks. They built great stamp mills that dwarfed the mortars and pestles of the individual miners, and the *arrastras* of the Mexicans. The stamp mills were really just giant mortars and pestles. Instead of using a plodding mule to do the work the stamp mill used a steam engine.

When the rocks were first brought out of the mine, men with huge hammers pounded them until they were no larger than a fist. These smaller

An arrastra was a simple device powered by a slow-moving mule, and it didn't require a lot of capital to operate.

Large mining operations like this one required a great deal of capital, and companies of business and professional men were formed to provide it.

rocks were then shoveled onto a slanted board where, with the aid of an overhead hose, they were washed down to an iron plate. Another cast iron plate weighing from five hundred to one thousand pounds was suspended some thirteen inches above the rocks. When a lever released the heavy plate it would crash down on the rocks again and again.

Meanwhile a continual flow of water washed the crushed rocks through a fine sieve. The debris small enough to pass through the sieve would flow down a Long-Tom-type sluicing channel from which the gold could be retrieved. Rocks not fine enough to go through the sieve were returned for a second crushing. A single steam engine was capable of operating a whole battery of stamp mills. And the racket they made in the once quiet valley must have been deafening.

The stamp mills would do the work of crushing the quartz. But miners were still needed to bring it up from deep underground and to perform the various other operations that quartz mining required. Men who had formerly prospected for placer gold and who were now unable to make a living at it took jobs with the big companies.

Soon quartz mining spread to neighboring Nevada City, and from there outward wherever the mother lode exposed her presence. With the steady work provided by the mining companies, many miners were now able to build permanent homes and settle down with their families. But none of these advantages could ever replace for them the thrill of that magical moment when gold appeared in the bottom of a pan or cradle or Long Tom. Those adventurous and footloose enough to follow their dream would continue the search, no matter how wild and remote the place might be.

A miner shovels small rocks onto the slanted board of a stamp mill. The rocks are washed down to an iron plate, where they are pounded even smaller by another overhead plate.

chapter 13

Women Arrive at the Camps

THE FIRST SHIPS LEAVING THE EAST COAST for California were filled exclusively with men. But as time went by, the rule was relaxed for women who wanted to join their husbands, some bringing their children with them. Special quarters were set up to accommodate these women. Also among them were some single girls, beguiled by the thought of finding rich husbands in the land of gold and plenty.

Once the women arrived in San Francisco, they were assured of finding work to support themselves until their husbands invited them to come to the camps and join them. Some of the women made a good living running boardinghouses. Others became seamstresses, or housekeepers in established homes, or nurses in the hospitals.

Young, unmarried girls without much experience could find work, too, but usually it was of a menial kind. Some who had come with the expectation of immediately snagging a rich husband turned up their noses at drudgery. They drifted into the entertainment world. As "fancy girls" they were employed in dance halls to provide men with partners. In gambling halls they presided over card games. In saloons they tended bar or served drinks.

Most of the miners weren't interested in these girls. They longed for the orderliness of their old life, for the presence of "respectable women" like the mothers or

Miners give a joyful welcome to the "decent" young wife who is joining her husband at his camp.

sisters, aunts or sweethearts they had left behind. When the miners of the little town of Columbia learned that a "decent" woman was finally coming to their town to join her husband, they went wild with excitement. They dropped their work at the diggings to lop off fresh pine branches from the surrounding trees and put up leafy arches along the length of Main Street. Then, led by an improvised band, they marched out to escort her proudly to her new home.

The same enthusiasm greeted other "decent women," some with children, who started arriving at mining camps. Wherever these women showed up, they brought a feminine touch with them, if it was only to spread a bright calico cloth over the crude log table in the shanty she would now call home.

The women brought another feminine skill to their husbands, who were weary of the monotonous diet of hardtack and salt pork. Now, coming in tired and hungry from a long day at the diggings, husbands were beguiled by the tantalizing odor of baking biscuits and frying sausages, of broiling beef and lentil soup. It was enough to draw other hungry men flocking for a sniff, perhaps a taste.

Some women put their cooking skills to good use by serving home-cooked meals to miners at a stiff price. Soon they had earned enough to set up a small restaurant or boardinghouse. Boardinghouses run by husband and wife teams or by single women began appearing in many mining camps. Other women began laundering men's shirts. Often a wife made more money washing shirts at a dollar apiece than

Women who accepted camp life learned quickly about the hardships they would have to face in the sudden weather changes of the Sierra Nevada. Here a miner leads his wife and her floundering horse to shelter through a driving snowstorm.

Women made a difference. With their arrival in Hangtown, it was transformed into a more respectable place, with schools and churches and organizations to try and combat drinking and gambling. The women of Hangtown campaigned to change the town's name to a more respectable "Placerville."

her husband could bring home from his diggings.

The presence of women served to soften the rough edges of the mining towns. The arrival of children at Hangtown meant a schoolhouse had to be built and a schoolteacher hired, probably a woman. The schoolhouse was followed by a church to get rid of lawless Sundays, or so it was hoped. Then a temperance league was added to combat the saloons.

Hangtown had now achieved so much respectability that teenage girls in long, dainty dresses could stroll arm in arm down the main street without any fear of being harassed. The admiring miners even made up a song to honor them. Titled "The Hangtown Gals," one version began:

> *They're dreadful shy of forty-niners*
> *Turn their noses up at miners . . .*

In 1850, Hangtown citizens, ashamed of their uncouth name, again changed it. Hangtown became a dignified Placerville.

Downieville was another mining town that strove for respectability, but without Hangtown's success. It had been the town's custom to greet every holiday with a drunken orgy. It was such an orgy that had led to the lynching of the beautiful Juanita, and this still troubled the conscience of the Downieville miners. This was why in 1855 they were determined to greet the coming Independence Day with complete sobriety. They invited a renowned temperance speaker, Miss Sarah Pellet, to give the principal oration. In the days before she came, they launched a crusade with such ardor that the entire body of miners joined the Sons of Temperance Society. By the time Independence Day came around, the saloons were empty.

Hundreds of miners gathered for Miss Pellet's anticipated address. Unfortunately, she was preceded by another speaker, whose job was to introduce her. Instead of giving a brief preamble, he droned on and on until the impatient miners began firing their pistols into the air in protest.

One of those who became especially annoyed even gave a blast from his shotgun. At this, the speaker pulled out his own gun and the two engaged in a duel. It ended when the speaker was killed where he stood. Miss Pellet fled without giving her stirring speech, and the miners flocked to the saloons, which did as brisk a business as on any other Fourth in memory.

Some of the women who came to California were more adventurous than domestic. One of these was Louisa Smith Clappe, who in 1849 left New Haven, Connecticut, with her physician husband, Fayette, to travel by sea to San Francisco. By 1851 her husband, whose health could not endure San Francisco's thick fogs, decided to locate his practice in the remote mining camp of Rich Bar. Louisa soon followed him there.

Signing her name Dame Shirley, Louisa wrote her sister voluminous letters telling of her experiences at Rich Bar. She described how she made the long journey there, traveling by stagecoach and river steamer and finally on the back of a mule that plodded warily along a treacherous trail. From the top of a cliff she finally looked down into the canyon through which the North Fork of the Feather River ran. Along the bank below her she saw the straggling row of tents, hovels, and log cabins that made up the town.

Dame Shirley spent a year and a half in Rich Bar, half terrified but at the same time exhilarated by the raucous behavior of the miners. In a letter to her sister she detailed the events that occurred during three tumultuous weeks in July of 1852: "murders, fearful accidents, bloody deaths, a mob, whippings, a hanging, an attempt at suicide, and a fatal duel."

Whatever the behavior of the men toward one another, they were always protective of the few women who had joined their husbands. Dame Shirley wrote of enjoying the company of these women. Among the simple pleasures were quiet walks through the fragrant pine woods, gathering armloads of wildflowers.

Dame Shirley's stay in Rich Bar was not destined to last for long, however. As with every other mining town, Rich Bar's existence depended on gold. When the gold played out, the town died unless it had some other reason for existence. In the fall of 1852 the miners' pans at Rich Bar were no longer showing color. By November they were packing up their belongings and leaving.

Miners were more likely to build cabins after their wives joined them. It was in a well-built cabin like this one where Dame Shirley and her husband spent two years at the remote mining camp of Rich Bar.

A freezing rain had given way to snow by the time the Clappe were ready to go. From her doorstep, Shirley took a last look at the soft snow drifting down the silent street, dusting the "calico hovels, the shingle palaces, the ramoras, pretty arborlike places composed of green boughs" that had once been so full of life.

She was sensing the loss of something she had never experienced before. It was the freedom to do as she pleased, unrestricted by the stern rules of etiquette and dress that had governed her every move in formal New England.

"My heart is heavy at the thought of departing forever from this place," she wrote her sister. "I *like* this wild and barbarous life. I leave it with regret."

Entertainment

THE GAMBLING HALLS WEREN'T USED JUST FOR gambling. They were also social halls where the miners could gather in the evenings. It was there that friendships were formed.

Most of the friendships were temporary because the miners were a restless lot. On the spur of the moment they might drop one claim and be off to search for a richer one elsewhere. This meant that each time a miner moved he might find himself among utter strangers—unless he belonged to a fraternity with widespread chapters where he could strike up new friendships and get trustworthy advice. Many miners joined such fraternities as the Masons and the Odd Fellows. But the most popular fraternity in gold-mining country was one called E Clampus Vitus. E Clampus Vitus, a fraternity that is still popular today, was widespread in gold rush times. With tongue in cheek it claimed to have been founded in 4000 B.C. in the Garden of Eden by Adam, its first patriarch. As stated in its bylaws, the purpose of the fraternity was "the care of widows and orphans." But in the mining communities, at least, the members seem to have been chiefly concerned with having fun, making new friends, and exchanging stories and ideas with one another.

Valuable as the fraternities were to the miners, they couldn't ease the feelings of loneliness that were especially strong during the holiday seasons. Christmas and the Fourth of July were the most difficult. These were the times when social events were held back home—parades, banquets, lavish balls.

"SATURDAY NIGHT IN THE MINES"
BUFFALO BREWING CO. SACRAMENTO, CALIF.

Craving the glamour of the balls they had once attended back home, the miners in some camps put on their own riotous balls using male partners.

Parades, patriotic speeches, and banquets were easy to arrange. But nothing could take the place of a ball and waltzing with a glamorous partner. Before the arrival of women at the remote town of Weaverville, the men decided to hold their own ball. They paired off with one another, using a simple standard to determine male or female partners. Men with ragged, grimy clothes would be the males. Those with the neater clothes would be the females. The ball went forward. The music played, the men danced. They pranced around with a lot of rowdy spirit. But no matter how loud the music and how boisterous the prancing, it was never quite satisfactory, because a man was still a man.

By the end of 1852 some thirty-two "respectable women" had arrived in Weaverville, and the idea of putting on a real ball took fire again. This time women and men worked together to make the arrangements.

A ball! A ball! A ball with real women! The word spread up and down the mining camps. The exciting news reached the town of Shasta some forty miles away. And four daring women who lived there put on the party dresses they had brought from home, mounted balking mules, and rode to Weaverville over some of the roughest, most hazardous trails in the Sierra Nevada.

The men now had a problem. They wanted to match the women's party gowns with formal attire of their own—dress coat, white vest, boiled shirt, and polished boots. All the men had boots. Unfortunately, only a fraction of them possessed dress attire. The problem was solved when the owners of the outfits agreed to share them.

Each miner was allotted his turn on the dance floor. After an hour or so he would retire to the back room and pass the formal outfit on to the next man. No matter the fit—too big, too tight, pants and sleeves too long or too short—every man had his turn.

Since Weaverville had the reputation of being one of the wildest cities on the Mother Lode, some of the party goers were afraid that this evening, like so many others, would end in a brawl. But as one astonished celebrant observed, "It went off first-rate. I was afraid there would be a row of some kind, but everyone behaved themselves with propriety."

The ball was so successful that people started talking of putting on another on Independence Day. And eager miners, wanting to perform better on the dance floor, began begging the women to give them dancing lessons.

The miners also enjoyed performances of all kinds and provided theaters for

The Jenny Lind Theater was the largest, most imposing theater in San Francisco, a must for visiting performers until 1852, when it was bought by the city, remodeled, and turned into City Hall, a function it still fulfills today.

A portrait of Lola, her glamorous beauty once the toast of European royalty.

this purpose. The first mining town to have a real theater was Nevada City. The theater was a large, barnlike building on Main Street, equipped with a stage, boxes for the elite, a pit for the orchestra, and a gallery for common folk. Theaters in other towns were just ramshackle shanties or large tents equipped with a stage and seating for the audience.

The mining town theaters began by putting on their own performances. Before the arrival of women, males played both male and female parts. Then, as San Francisco became a booming city, rich with gold, worldwide acting troupes started including it in their tours. Once the troupes were in the city, many of them decided to add a detour into the mining camps.

Visits to gold country were a special lure to performers whose acts were beginning to fall flat in the big cities. In the camps, actors could be sure of a wild reception, thunderous applause accompanied by hoots and hollers of admiration, along with the stamping of heavy boots. And a shower of silver coins and packets of gold dust would rain down on the stage.

The miners preferred female to male performers, especially if the women were young and beautiful and were accomplished dancers, musicians, or vocalists. One of the most notorious of these performers was a dancer named Lola Montez, the alias of a young woman from Limerick, Ireland. Lola had been the toast of Europe, where she had married two husbands without the benefit of a divorce. She had also been the mistress of a series of men, including Prince Ludwig I of Bavaria.

Lola's fame sprang from the dance she performed at the end of a drama called *Tarantula.* The dance depicted the heroine caught in a nest of vicious spiders that she was attempting to shake off. The spiders were made of cork and wire. As she danced, they bounced around her, held to her short skirt by elastic thread.

At first Lola's dance was considered delightfully risque in the European cities, but as time brought more sophistication, her dance began to seem outdated. So in 1851 Lola sailed for New York. Her performances were greeted enthusiastically in New York, Boston, and Philadelphia. But that didn't last. Reviews became critical and audiences lukewarm. Lola came to San Francisco to change her luck, but that city wasn't much interested either. Sometimes people even began laughing at her performances.

Embarrassed and humiliated, Lola retreated to the mining towns to energize her fading career and escape her latest husband. She decided to settle in Grass Valley, by this time a town of some three thousand people, a bustling, noisy place drowned in the constant clank and clatter of the stamp mills that ran day and night.

It was probably Grass Valley's sizable European population, with its large percentage of French, that attracted Lola. She had spent some pleasant time in Paris entertaining

In her "Spider Dance," a coy Lola works her way out of the nest of tarantulas by whirling round and round in double-quick time, causing her short skirt to billow provocatively around her.

A grown-up Lotta Crabtree. She became a world-famous performer, but she never married, and at her death bestowed her wealth on charitable causes.

guests at fashionable parties. She planned to do the same in Grass Valley. She bought a bungalow in town and prepared to hold court there. She made friends with the Crabtree family, who owned the boardinghouse next door. Lola immediately took an interest in the Crabtree's little six-year-old daughter, Lotta. Lotta had already proved herself an accomplished dancer and singer. She could set the miners to stamping their feet with delight whenever she performed her Irish jig, her red curls bouncing, her tiny shillelagh twirling.

It is said that Lola taught little Lotta some of her own dances, for which Lotta became famous in later years. But whether this was true or not, it wasn't long before Lola became the subject of controversy, even in Grass Valley, where she had been so enthusiastically welcomed. She enjoyed shocking people by walking down Main Street in low-cut dresses, smoking cigars. And her flamboyant fights with those who crossed her were the talk of the town. She demanded unquestioning loyalty even from the two grizzly bears she kept as pets. When one of them bit her, she shot it on the spot.

By 1855 the tempestuous Lola, having succeeded in shedding her last husband, was ready to leave Grass Valley for distant Australia. She had become so fond of little Lotta that, according to gossip, she offered to take the child with her. But the Crabtrees wouldn't allow it. They had already arranged a tour of the mines for their talented daughter, who they hoped would be their meal ticket in days to come.

Lotta was one of a number of little girls who performed for the miners. Eight-year-old Susan Robinson, who sang and danced, was another. The Bateman sisters—Kate, age ten, and Ellen, age eleven—toured the mining towns, performing the leads in several Shakespearean plays. Wherever they went, the girls were always received with enthusiasm and affection, for they reminded the homesick miners of their own distant daughters and sons.

The Bateman sisters, dressed in costume for a performance of Shakespeare's play King Richard III: Ellen (left) as evil Richard, Kate (right) as Richmond.

chapter 15

The Mountain Tribes

FEW OF THE 1848 GOLD SEEKERS HAD PAID MUCH attention to the Native Americans who had started panning for gold, now that they had learned the value the white man placed on it. Gold was so plentiful then that no one was concerned about the little the tribes were gleaning. But by the time the forty-niners arrived most of the easily found placer gold had been harvested. The newcomers, who had traveled so far with such great expectations, were bitterly disappointed. When they saw those they regarded as mere savages hunting for gold that they felt was rightfully theirs their resentment against the Native Americans grew.

Sensing the animosity of the newcomers the Native Americans tried to melt into the crowd by dressing in the same outfits as the American miners—flannel shirts, wool pants, slouch hats or, if they were women, cast-off western-style dresses. But whatever they did the prejudice against them kept growing until the least spark was likely to set things off. That spark flared in the mining town of Volcano.

It began when a miner realized his pick was missing and immediately suspected one of the local tribesmen of having taken it. Accompanied by a group of his friends the miner went to the tribal chief to complain about the supposed theft. The chief promised to search for the missing pick, saying if he found it he would return it at once. He raced off to look for it, determined to keep the peace, but he hadn't gone far when the crack of a rifle shattered the day and the chief fell dead. A former Texas Ranger, Rod Stowell, had fired the shot. He explained that he thought the man was running away.

A Native-American woman, wearing a white woman's cast-off clothing, pans for gold. In an effort to appear inconspicuous women as well as men began wearing western clothes.

Rumors spread fast. The Native Americans, who before had been on good terms with the miners, were outraged at the shooting and began threatening war. The Texas Ranger and his friends had to come up with some kind of story to cover themselves. They told the other miners that they'd been attacked by a band of the local savages who had murdered one of them before Stowell, the hero, had managed to drive them off by shooting their chief. Without checking the facts, the whole body of miners armed themselves and marched to the tribal camp, taking it by surprise. They drove off the occupants in a heated but uneven exchange—guns against bows and arrows—that cost them the life of one of their own people. This incident was immediately dubbed the Volcano War.

It was only later that the miners learned the truth about the chief's death. Infuriated by the reckless action of the ranger and the lies that followed, they drove Stowell and his companions out of the camp. But by this time it was too late to appease the growing tide of anger that was sweeping through the mountain tribes. They saw the shooting of the chief and the destruction of a whole village as just one more brutal action by the white man against their people.

For hundreds of years the tribes had lived in these mountains in peace with their neighbors. Now these arrogant newcomers were invading their homeland and destroying the limited food supplies on which they depended. Meadowlands rich with grasses bearing edible seeds were being torn apart. In the forests the wild game was being hunted down by the strangers, who were also diverting the channels of rivers, the home of freshwater fish. To get lumber for their Long Toms, sluices, and cabins, the invaders were chopping the stands of oak trees that produced the acorns that formed the basic food supplies of the tribes.

Now they had to face the winter of 1849 with granaries only half full. The cold came early, bringing heavy snows and bitter rains. With their wives and children suffering near-starvation, the tribesmen had no other recourse than to begin raiding the supply mule trains and robbing solitary travelers of their provisions.

Winter had clamped down on the miners, too. Unable to work their digs during that season, many left to spend their idle time in such towns as Sacramento, where they frequented the saloons. It was in the Sacramento saloons that they heard about the raids. The miners were suddenly roused. They would, they promised, avenge all those thefts. It would be something adventurous to do, something to prove their mettle and at the same time give them a break from days of boredom.

The miners held meeting after meeting to organize the raids they planned. The drunken ones greeted each decision with a roar of approval. The sober ones objected. This, they said, was needless violence against a starving people. They voted for peace but were shouted down.

The popular *Sacramento Transcript* called the raids a just war and claimed the backing of the town's merchants, who wanted "those Injuns" stopped. Other papers pointed out that "those" Indians weren't doing that much damage, and the real reason the merchants wanted war was to make a quick profit selling the miners military goods.

The miners carried out their raids zealously. They burned villages and granaries. They chased Native Americans from the trails, killing a number of them in the process. Finally spring brought fair weather and the miners went back to their digs, but their

A young woman gathers acorns, which she stores in the basket she carries on her back.

Women cooking meals outdoors in front of their homes.

actions had roused the anger of the mountain tribes, and rumors of a general uprising by them began spreading fear throughout gold country.

In the north bands of warriors started attacking isolated pioneer homes, ferry landings, and tiny settlements. Even in the more settled coastal areas, travelers passing through the Santa Ynez mountains behind Santa Barbara were sometimes brought down by a solitary tribal scout armed now with a rifle.

In the summer of 1850 tribes in the Mariposa region openly proclaimed their intention of driving all the gold diggers from their ancestral lands. They struck the first blow in the foothills surrounding Mariposa, where some warriors killed several white miners and raided some trading posts.

The furious miners responded by marching on the nearest village and setting fire to the dwellings. Made of reeds, grass, and tree bark, the thatching on them burst into flames. As the occupants rushed out, the miners shot them down, killing twenty-four men, women, and children, among them the chief. The bloody massacre was dubbed the Mariposa War.

One of the last uprisings took place around Weaverville. It was launched by a

The arrival of great numbers of forty-niners into the Sierra Nevada wilderness destroyed much of the early Native-Americans' culture and decimated their numbers. Clashes between whites and Indians were never evenly matched. No matter how brave the Indian warriors were, they could not win using bows and arrows against the guns of the newcomers.

tribe that the miners had contemptuously nicknamed "Diggers" because they dug up roots for food.

The raids reached a crisis in May of 1852 when a roving band of warriors killed the butcher of Weaverville, who was driving some cattle to town. The sheriff gathered a posse together and marched to the nearest village. There he and his men killed more than a hundred Native Americans, leaving only two or three small children alive. The senseless and brutal action, which the miners dignified with the word *war*, cowed the chief of the tribe responsible for the butcher's murder. Toward the end of 1852 he went to Weaverville to sign a treaty with the whites.

It was hoped the chief's surrender would mark an end to any serious threat from the Native Americans. But the anger of the tribes was now so great that whenever the opportunity arose, they would attack, then melt away into the silent heart of the mountains that they knew so well.

With time, however, the raids became more and more infrequent. The Native Americans were losing a battle to enemies far more dangerous than any weapon—the white man's diseases. Small pox, cholera, dysentery, and measles were spreading throughout the scattered villages of the Sierra Nevada, bringing death with them.

chapter 16

The Foreign Gold Seekers

THE 1849 GOLD RUSH BROUGHT IN TENS OF THOUSANDS of people from around the world. There were Chinese, Hawaiian Islanders, Mexicans, Chileans, Australians, Canadians, British, French, and Germans. Though California was now a possession of the United States, the governor was allowing everyone who came free access to the gold fields.

The newly arrived Americans were angry about this. They had mortgaged their homes and farms and drained their savings, expecting to make a quick fortune and return home before the families they had

Various nationalities can be seen in this horse auction: American miners on the far left; two Chinese beside them; on the far right, a well-dressed black man; next to him, several Mexicans; and behind the horse, a Frenchman in a beret.

left behind faced poverty. Now they were finding that many of the best gold deposits had been taken over by foreigners who had managed to get there first.

The Argonauts who came by way of Panama were especially angry at the Chileans. Great numbers of them had boarded American ships that stopped at the Chilean seaport of Valparaiso on their way north to San Francisco. By the time the ships arrived at Panama, they were too crowded to take on the Americans who were waiting there. Sometimes it would be months before they could book passage.

When the Argonauts finally did arrive, some of them made their way to the gold diggings at Mokelumne Hill, rumored to have rich placer gold deposits. When they got there, they found Chileans were working the deposits. The frustrated Americans began jumping the Chilean claims. The Chileans fought back. Several men on both sides were killed before the Americans finally drove the Chileans off the hill and took over their claims. The Americans called this the Chilean War.

The Chileans fled to San Francisco where they were attacked by a group that called

Mokelumne Hill miners at work. At first, peons brought over by a wealthy Chilean worked the numerous claims he had registered in their names. The slave status of the peons enraged the forty-niners.

The Chileans found no better reception in San Francisco. A vigilante group called the Hounds made it their goal to drive all foreigners out of California, and conducted periodic raids on the foreign settlements in San Francisco, beating, looting, and killing.

itself the Hounds. The Hounds were a criminal gang whose goal was to chase all non-Anglo-Saxon foreigners out of California. Until another vigilante group drove the Hounds out of San Francisco they continued to conduct periodic rampages in the city's foreign settlements, looting, burning, killing, striking terror in their victims.

Meanwhile back at Mokelumne Hill the French had begun to worry that the Americans would storm their camp next. They armed themselves, raised an earthen bulwark in front of their gold digs, and as a last defiant act flew the French tricolor over it. It's not known whether or not the Americans had ever planned to attack the French camp, but the sight of that foreign flag flying on United States soil roused them to fury. One hundred strong, they stormed the French fort, as they called it. They tore down the flag and stole a large amount of gold, then left proclaiming victory. They called this escapade the French War.

By this time American miners in all the gold fields were complaining loudly to the government about the way foreigners were taking over the gold fields. In June of 1850 the state legislature responded by passing a law

A French license to mine gold, the fee written in French francs.

A Chinese miner arrives at the gold fields. At first, the Chinese, with their long pigtails and strange apparel, were a source of amusement to the Americans.

requiring foreigners to pay a monthly fee of thirty-five dollars.

Foreign miners were outraged. Most of them were clearing little more than ten dollars a week and could not possibly meet the tax. They tried banding together to fight off the tax collector. But this didn't help, because the collector simply seized their property and auctioned it off to get his fee.

The Chinese suffered most from the new law. Since they couldn't understand the language, they didn't know what was being demanded of them. They just stood patiently by while the collector appropriated their belongings.

The Mexicans in the town of Sonora were more militant. Sonora had once been a tranquil Mexican village, but when gold deposits were discovered nearby, Mexicans and Americans began swarming to the area. The population exploded. The little village became a large town of some five thousand people. The old Spanish-style houses were joined by western-style frame houses. Saloons and gambling dens multiplied. Mexican fandango halls, which featured spirited fandango dancers, increased in number. The town became a bustling community as wild as any other gold mining town.

In June of 1850 the tax collector arrived. Angry Mexicans armed themselves, vowing they would pay no tax. Armed Americans sided with the tax collector. The standoff continued for days. Then suddenly it was broken by another crisis. A group of furious American miners rushed into town dragging along four terrified men, three Native Americans and a Mexican.

"Murder! Murder!" shouted their captors.

A mob quickly gathered. Keeping tight hold of their prisoners, their captors explained that the men had been found burning the corpses of two Americans whom they had just killed. At this the crowd went wild and began yelling, "Justice! Justice!" In an instant a jury was picked. It gave a quick verdict—death by hanging.

The sleepy, little Mexican town of Sonora was transformed into a roaring gold-rush town.

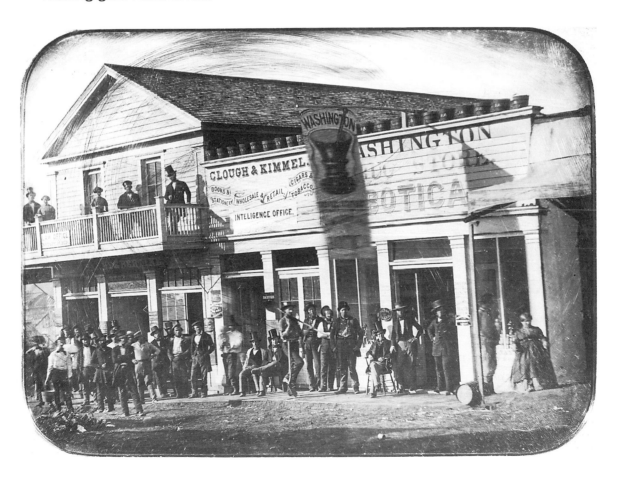

97

The crowd roared its approval. Ropes ending in nooses appeared. The nooses were looped around the necks of the four men, and the ropes were tossed over the limbs of a nearby tree. The Mexican was hoisted up just as the newly elected sheriff and his deputy burst through the mob. The sheriff cut down the Mexican and took the nooses from the necks of his three companions. He escorted his prisoners to jail, promising them they would have a fair trial.

This might have ended the crisis, except for the next bit of bad news. A crowd of a hundred or more Mexicans was just about to enter the town. Was their purpose to rescue the jailed men? Before the mob could act, the quick-thinking sheriff sent a posse of ten well-armed men to round up the suspected rescuers and herd them into a corral to await questioning.

A Native American binding a corpse for burning or burial.

The next day the four accused men were brought to trial. They explained that they had come upon the bodies of the dead Americans. Out of compassion for the dead, the Native Americans, assisted by the Mexican, had burned the bodies. According to their ancient belief, only by doing this could the tortured souls of the dead know peace.

As for the bewildered Mexicans in the corral, they explained that their only purpose in coming there was to dig for gold. Upon hearing the explanations, the sheriff released all the prisoners. The hundred or so Mexicans had had enough. They turned around and headed back for the safety of Mexico. Many Mexicans living in Sonora joined them. By September more than three-fourths of Sonora's population had left. The once lively town was now as quiet as a ghost town.

The Americans began taking over the Mexican gold claims, but it was a dangerous thing to do. Some Mexicans had stayed behind to become outlaws. Silent as shadows, they roamed at will through the American camps stealing back the gold that had once been theirs. American miners slept with their packets of gold dust under their pillows and their loaded pistols beside them. No matter! When they woke in the morning, they would find both gone. Daytime was as threatening as the night. Everywhere was the threat of violent death. In one week along eleven unsolved murders were reported.

The nearby mining towns of Angel's Camp and San Andreas were seething. Fierce clashes between Americans and Mexicans were made worse by the appearance of the hated tax collector. It was obvious that the exorbitant tax was doing more harm than good. The following year the legislature repealed it, and a more modest three-dollar fee was substituted.

But the damage was already done. Out of the turmoil at San Andreas an avenging angel suddenly flashed into California history and folklore. His name was Joaquín Murrieta, a slender, soft-spoken, mustached Mexican. He is pictured as a dashing figure in a gold-embroidered jacket and jaunty hat flaunting a bright feather. Beside him rides his girlfriend, a young senorita dressed in boys' clothes. They are accompanied by two lieutenants, Valenzuela and "Three-Fingered" Garcia, along with a gang of the fiercest outlaws in the area.

From San Andreas, Murrieta and his gang rode through the gold camps of the southern mother lode, robbing, burning, killing. Only Mexican rancheros and

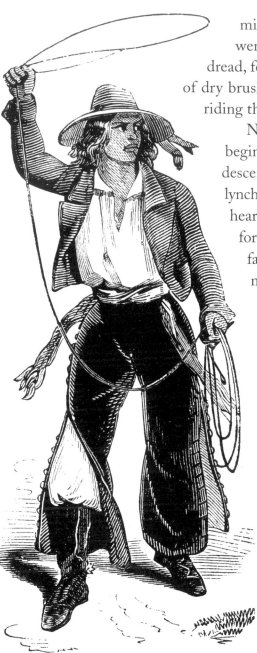

Mexican cowboys working ranches were safe from Murrieta's raids.

mining camps were safe from him. All others were fair game. Travelers on lonely roads went in dread, fearing that every shadow, every soft crackling of dry brush were signs that Joaquín and his men were riding their way.

Nobody really knows the true story of Murrieta's beginnings. Legend says that American miners descended on Murrieta's home in San Andreas, lynched his innocent brother, raped Joaquín's sweetheart, and whipped Joaquín himself, leaving him for dead. Joaquín recovered. Vowing to avenge his family's honor, he spent years tracking down the men responsible and finally killed them.

So goes the legend. Whatever the real cause for his rampages, Murrieta managed to evade every posse, every trap set for him. From 1851 to 1853 he seemed invincible. Then in 1853 the state legislature offered a large reward to anyone who could lead the posse to Joaquín's hiding place. A follower betrayed him and led a posse to his hideout. In the ensuing battle, Murrieta and his lieutenants were killed. Murrieta's head and Garcia's three-fingered hand were sent to San Francisco as proof. Preserved in alcohol, they were kept for years in the old San Francisco Museum.

But not everyone was convinced it was really Murrieta's head, since the bloody raids continued. Dead or alive, Murrieta still rode over California hills and valleys, the hero of Mexicans, the scourge of Anglo-Saxons.

Joaquín Murrieta rides like an avenging myth through the hearts and minds of California Mexicans of yesteryear.

The Express Riders

"I AM GETTING VERY OLD, MOTHER," WROTE ARGONAUT Albert Francisco from one of California's remote mining camps. "You would hardly know me. My hair is quite gray. This country wears a man out very fast."

What a change the tone of that letter is from the early days of 1849, when young men, their faces bright with the dream of sudden riches, left home to make their fortune. Many of those men now found themselves trapped. All they could do was keep at their diggings, with the forlorn hope that they would strike it rich or at least manage to scrape together enough gold to pay for their passage home or to send something back to their families. What they missed most were letters from home. The only ones reaching them were those brought by way of friends, or travelers just passing through.

Up until February of 1849 there wasn't even a United States post office in all of California. Then a postal agent, William Van Vorhees, was dispatched with orders to open post offices in five California towns. By June the number had been increased to thirty-four. But these towns were situated in coastal and central California. They were of little use to the great numbers of miners in the Sierra Nevada.

Marooned in tiny camps tucked away into corners of the mountains, with no letters from home to cheer them up, the men felt utterly abandoned. Meanwhile, California express companies were receiving pouches of mail freighted to them by their eastern counterparts. With no way to deliver them, letters for the scattered mining towns they were piling up everywhere.

Nothing could deter the express rider on his mad dash to isolated mining camps. When mule trains blocked his passage on narrow trails, he often forged his own way through the wild and treacherous terrain.

Enter the express riders—young men looking for a way to earn a living. Some approached express offices, offering to deliver the mail that was addressed to remote mining camps. Others preferred to work as individual carriers. To avoid a clash with the United States Postal Service, some carriers asked to be sworn in as postal clerks before going to the express offices to collect the mail for delivery. Others

An express rider urges his horse on to reach a mining camp with his precious load of mail.

ignored the post office. The earliest express riders charged as much as four dollars to deliver a letter. As competition grew this fee was cut to two dollars, and then to one dollar. To miners strapped for money, even this was a high price to pay.

The express riders traveled by horse or mule or even afoot. However they went, they took their job seriously. To get to the camps as quickly as possible, they blazed hazardous shortcuts through thorny thickets and dense forests. They scrambled up and down steep ravines and crossed wild rivers. They faced hungry wolves, and evaded fierce grizzlies and roving bands of warriors.

At every camp the eager miners cheered when an express rider appeared. They crowded around him, jostling one another to get the letter from home that would brighten their day.

Express rider Pilsbury Hodgkin's steed was a rare white mule. At the sight of white against the white of snowdrifts, the shout would go up, "Here comes Chips! Here comes Chips!" and the rush was on.

Sweet Charley Schaeffer boasted in his youthful pride that no storm, no flood, no blizzard piling up high drifts could stop him from delivering his mail on schedule. Then came a day of torrential rains. Charley was warned to give it up, but out he went. Only three miles from Weaverville he disappeared. A rescue party found his mule and saddlebags beside a flooding creek. Farther downstream they found Charley's broken body sprawled among the rocks. He had been battered to death by the swift-running current. Charley was just one of the express riders who died while making sure the mail was delivered.

Ferries like this one, tended by only two or three ferrymen, were a temptation to bands of roving warriors. Sometimes it was the express rider galloping at full speed who managed to spread the alarm of impending danger.

Some of the riders were especially enterprising. One of these was Alexander Todd. Not only did he carry the mail into the mountains and gold out of them, he also managed to be in San Francisco on the days the mail steamers arrived. He was always the first to row out to the incoming ship. There he purchased all the old

newspapers the passengers had brought with them, often getting two to three hundred from a single ship. He would pay a dollar per paper. In the mining towns he would sell the papers at eight dollars apiece. No matter how dog-eared and out-of-date they were, they still brought welcome news from faraway hometowns.

Presently Todd had saved enough capital to rent an office in town and equip it with an iron safe, where he began storing the gold entrusted to him by the miners, charging them one percent a month for the service.

Todd's business grew so large that he took on partners and hired clerks. Unfortunately during the gold rush days the taint of gold seemed to invade almost every transaction. Honest Todd was betrayed by his thieving clerks, who stole from him shamelessly in sums that ranged from forty thousand to seventy thousand dollars.

News from home could bring a smile or tears.

chapter 18

Banking the Gold

THE 1849 GOLD RUSH STIRRED THE IMAGINATION OF twenty-three-year-old Daniel Dale Haskell. He was a clerk in the offices of the Alvin Adams Express Company, operating out of New York City. Adams was the successful owner of a wide-reaching express and banking concern that carried cargoes of various kinds throughout the eastern half of the United States.

Young Haskell wanted to open an office in San Francisco to handle some of the cargoes of gold dust, flakes, and nuggets that were already arriving by ship from the gold fields. Adams viewed Haskell's enthusiasm with a skeptical eye. Despite the quantities of gold now being shipped to the East Coast, he wasn't convinced it would be anything more than another fly-by-night venture.

However, Haskell was persuasive.

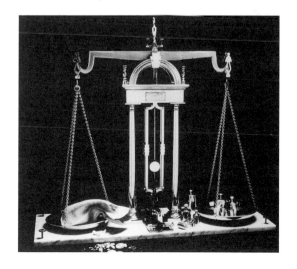

These elegant scales, with their precise weights, guaranteed the honesty of the banker who used them and were prominently displayed on his counter.

He was finally able to get Adams to grant his request and provide him with a modest capital so that he could open an office in San Francisco. But the still-cautious Adams warned Haskell that the California venture would be at most only a minor adjunct of the eastern firm.

Afire with excitement, young Haskell set out on the long sea voyage. He arrived in San Francisco in November 1849, and set up a modest office in a ramshackle building on Sacramento Street. Once settled, he placed an advertisement in the city newspapers. It read: "Express for New York, Boston and the principal towns of the New

Often a visit to one or another of the lavish saloons, like this one in San Francisco, dulled the wits of miners fresh from their solitary diggings. It made them easy prey to the many con men who promised high returns but cheated with false weights.

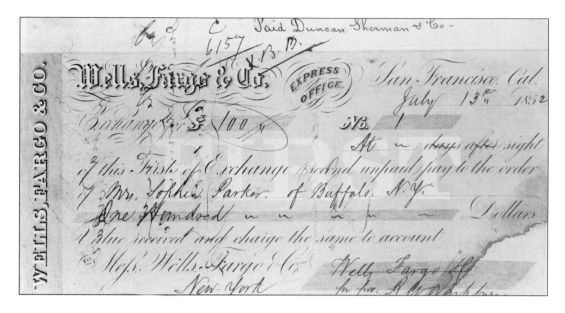

This bill of exchange had the same value as the gold that the holder had exchanged for it.

England states, Philadelphia, Baltimore, Washington, etc. Gold dust bought, also forwarded to any of the above places and bills of exchange given in any amounts. Letter bags made up and forwarded by special messengers in each of the steamers."

The promise to provide messengers to escort shipments on their long journey impressed San Franciscans. They had firsthand experience of how easy it was to steal unattended pouches of mail, especially if it was suspected they contained gold.

Haskell planned to do much more than just express mail. As his advertisement in the papers indicated, he also planned to act as an exchange office or bank, buying gold from clients and then shipping it to mints back east. There it would be stamped into twenty-dollar gold pieces about the size of a silver dime.

Since the gold the miners brought in would usually be mixed with silt, dust, and bits of gravel, the banks and exchange offices employed assayers, experts who would check samples of the ore and estimate the percentage of pure gold the whole contained.

After having the gold assayed, the banker or exchange manager would pay the client the equivalent of that amount either in cash or with a bill of exchange. The bill of exchange was much like today's certified check. For this service the banks would charge one or two percent. For another small monthly fee banks would store a client's valuables until he came to reclaim them. The storage space acted much like the safety deposit boxes modern banks provide.

Since the banks and exchange offices were not yet regulated in California, it was very easy for a dishonest assayer or clerk to shortchange an unsuspecting client. San Francisco swarmed with smooth-talking con men who set up exchange offices in the city. They made extravagant promises of rich returns in the advertisements they placed in newspapers. These ads often caught the eye of a miner fresh from his diggings. He would choose that exchange office, only to find himself cheated out of hundreds of dollars.

Clients soon learned how important it was to know the reputation of the bank or exchange office with whom they were dealing. And it was Haskell's connection with Adams and Company, already widely known for its integrity in the east, that brought in many of his clients. But Haskell knew that wasn't enough to ensure him a top spot in San Francisco's banking world. He would have to fight for a place among the already well-established banks, most of them local. He must have been aware, too, that the competition wouldn't end there. Sooner or later Wells Fargo and Company, a powerful competitor also known for its integrity, would be joining him on the coast.

The imposing Perrott building, into which Adams and Company moved, was built of granite blocks quarried in China and cut to precise measurements, so that each block would fit snugly against its neighbor. Since the blocks had all been numbered in Chinese, Chinese workers had to be brought over to erect the building.

chapter 19

Wells Fargo Arrives

HENRY WELLS AND WILLIAM G. Fargo, two of the directors of the newly formed American Express Company with headquarters in New York City, wanted to enter California in 1850. In December of 1851 American Express sent a representative to investigate the situation in California. He returned with a good report but American Express directors turned down the idea, so Wells and Fargo decided to form their own company to concentrate on California. They called it Wells, Fargo and Company. (In 1898 they dropped the comma between Wells and Fargo.)

Early in 1852 two Wells Fargo representatives arrived

Portraits of Henry Wells, prominent in the banking and express world in the East, and William G. Fargo, Wells's partner. Both men were among the directors of the American Express Company when they decided to set up their own express and banking service in the West.

Wells Fargo's agents took up offices in this modest brick building erected by Sam Brannan. It stood across the street from the imposing Perrott building that housed Adams and Company.

in California to open an office in San Francisco. They were Samuel F. Carter, in charge of transportation, and banker Reuben W. Washburn. They took a modest office on Montgomery Street. Across from them rose a massive building that now housed the Adams and Company offices. The grand new quarters of Adams and Company showed how quickly it had been able to rise in two and a half years. It was now among the top bankers in the city. In contrast, Wells Fargo would occupy the bottom rung on that ladder.

No matter! On July 1 Wells Fargo was ready to announce is presence with this advertisement in the San Francisco–based newspaper, the *Alta California:*

Wells Fargo is ready to undertake a general express forwarding agency.... The purchase of gold dust, bullion, and specie, also packages, parcels, and freight ... energetic and faithful messengers furnished with iron chests for the security of treasure and other valuable packages accompanying each express upon all their lines ...

They will immediately establish offices at all the principal towns in California and run messengers on their own account for the purpose of doing a general express business.

Carter and Washburn moved quickly. Within six months they had opened offices in some half dozen towns, including Sacramento, Auburn, and Marysville. They had carefully selected agents to manage the branch offices. One of the most efficient of the agents was twenty-one-year-old John Quincy Jackson, who wrote a proud letter to his mother about his important position:

> *"What I have to do is quite confining . . . staying in my office all day till 10 at night buying dust, forwarding and receiving packages of every kind . . . filling out drafts for the eastern mails in all sorts of sums, from $50 to $1,000 and drawing checks on the Offices below, when men wish to take cash to the cities as it is a great convenience to them to have a check instead . . . I have just come from the Post Office, from which I have got 100 letters to be forwarded to various parts of the country. On this I make $25 as my charge on each is 25 cents . . ."*

Jackson goes on to explain that personal expenses incurred, though heavy, still allow him to bring in a handsome income. Other duties included "the gold dust that has to be cleaned, scaled, and packed, ready to be forwarded in the morning . . . my books balanced . . . letters to be sorted—a list made of those received from Sacramento today."

The messenger escorts employed by Wells Fargo proved just as conscientious as the agents. Many of them were former express riders. It was their duty now to escort packages to and from the mines. Wherever rivers were available, the messenger would travel by paddle launch. Beyond the river he would go by stagecoach. The last lap over treacherous narrow trails would have to be done on horseback. The messenger was expected to make these runs as quickly as possible, because a reputation for being fast as well as reliable would bring business to the firm.

Getting there fast often meant being reckless. Californians were sporting people. There was nothing more exciting to them than watching a race between the river paddle steamers. Curious onlookers often lined the riverbanks to watch such races.

It was even more exciting when rival launches carried messengers from rival firms. Passengers on the launches liked to bet gold dust on the outcome of the races. They pressured the captains of the launches to increase the speed. That meant more steam. Sometimes the fires under the boilers would be stoked so high they became red-hot and in danger of exploding.

In June of 1851 the *New World*, racing down the Sacramento River, blew the top off her boiler, killing several people and badly burning others.

"We trust the steamboat racing will not be persevered in," a reporter for the *Alta California* wrote. "For if it be we shall very soon have some horrible catastrophe to chronicle . . ." Despite this warning, no one seemed interested in ending the races, and the explosions continued. Sometimes they took the life of a messenger and destroyed the pouch he carried.

The racing didn't end with the river steamers. Once a messenger left the river, usually in Sacramento, he needed to board a stagecoach for the next lap of his trip. There were some twelve to fifteen California-based stagelines all competing for passengers.

A traveler describes the chaotic scene at the departure site in Sacramento. The main street would be crowded with coaches and horses from the various lines, all heading for different destinations. Crowds of bewildered travelers would be milling around trying to find the coach they wanted to take. The general hubbub would be pierced by the strident shouts of hawkers touting their respective lines.

In all this confusion a messenger had to find his way to the right stagecoach before the passengers' places were filled. Even after he got aboard, the race would continue, because the messenger who got to the camps first would be the one to collect the mail and the gold and sell the newspapers he had gathered in San Francisco.

Too often paddle steamers racing against each other on the Sacramento River were pushed beyond the capacity of their steam boilers, causing explosions like this one on the *Jenny Lind*, with the tragic loss of passengers and cargo.

On bridges, many far flimsier than this rather fine one over the Merced River, stagecoaches were often delayed while passengers and their cargo were unloaded to lighten the coach during the hazardous crossing.

With a nudge from the messenger, the stagecoach driver understood that a race was on and played his part. He sent his horses flying under the sharp crack of his whip. Behind the horses the coach would sway dangerously from side to side, rattling and bumping along until the passengers were tumbled together in a jumble of arms and legs. Sometimes the wheels of the coach would become mired in thick mud. Then the passengers would have to pile out and push from behind while the horses pulled. At rickety bridges the passengers would have to get out and walk across, for fear their added weight would send bridge, horses, coach, and passengers tumbling into the waters below.

Sometimes the stagecoach drivers would rush through wooded areas, not because of a race but for fear of an ambush by either native warriors or bandits. Fortunately stagecoaches experienced few holdups, despite the great amounts of gold they carried.

When the messenger left the stagecoach, he would make his final lap on the

To carry the mail when snows were deep, a Wells Fargo employee hitched a crossbreed of Newfoundlands and Saint Bernards to a sled large enough to carry 250 pounds of weight as well as the ingenious express rider himself, J. B. Whiting.

back of a horse that was saddled and waiting for him at the last stop. Urging the horse on, the messenger would visit camp after camp, collect any packages, letters, and packets of gold, sell his papers, and be off to the next camp on his route.

Early in 1853, Adams and Company and Wells Fargo held a contest to see who would be the first to deliver the name of the newly elected president of the United States to all the mining towns.

Franklin Pierce just elected president of the United States! The news arrived by paddle steamer to San Francisco, and the race was on. Relays of skilled horsemen, galloping night and day, ate up the miles, passing on the news. Adams and Company won the race, covering 330 miles over treacherous trails to reach Weaverville in only seven hours. But the Wells Fargo firm, still new, wasn't far behind.

The speed at which business was being conducted in San Francisco astonished Henry Wells when he paid a visit to the city in February of 1853. He had always considered himself a progressive businessman, and was regarded as such on the East Coast, but now he wrote: "I am an old fogy here and considered entirely too slow for this market . . ." But, pleased with Wells Fargo's progress, he adds, " . . . We are now after seven months operation making money here." He went on to explain that the monthly estimates of Wells Fargo profits ranged from three to five thousand dollars.

Wells Fargo might have been considered a "one-horse bank," but it was moving up fast. At the same time, Adams and Company was slipping in esteem because of some shady practices. It seemed that Daniel Haskell had been turning over more and more of his bank's business to his manager Isaiah C. Woods. And there was some question about the way Woods was dealing with clients.

chapter 20

Boom

THE YEAR OF 1854 OPENED ON A BOOM IN CALIFORNIA. Large express and banking firms were still shipping out quantities of gold, though most of it was now coming from the deep-mining and hydraulic operations of big companies.

Visitors from around the world were flocking to San Francisco, attracted by business opportunities in the growing city. The United States government took note of San Francisco's growth and opened an assay office and mint there.

But despite its growing importance, San Francisco was in many ways still a raw frontier town, where sudden outbreaks of violence had in the past called vigilante groups into action. Most people lived in modest homes crowded together on the hillsides outside of town or in makeshift tents that still stood

Six times San Francisco went up in flames, fanned by fierce gales that swept in from the sea.

like mushrooms on less desirable slopes. The town's elite were the instant million-aires gold had created. They occupied stately homes in South Park and on Rincon Hill, the fashionable area of that time.

The city streets were still as muddy as ever though in the central district at least the sidewalks were now paved with wooden planks. Most of the impressive-looking buildings were still constructed of wooden frames covered by canvas painted to resemble massive stone. The city had been gutted by fire six times and had as quickly been rebuilt in the same flimsy manner.

However some architects were beginning to use more solid materials. The stone building that housed the Adams and Company firm and the brick building that housed Wells Fargo were both considered fireproof—as was the elegant Jenny Lind Theater which in 1852 was remodeled to serve as City Hall.

Ships from all over the world were still arriving in San Francisco Bay, their holds filled with merchandise—no longer shovels and picks and panning bowls. The elite on the hill wanted fashion-able clothes, gourmet foods, elegant furniture, oil paintings, chandeliers,

San Franciscans celebrated on the days ships bringing mail arrived in the harbor.

fine rugs and carpets, and carriages—all the things one needed to put on airs. More modest homes also required furnishings, foodstuffs, and clothing. And restaurant owners, saloon keepers, and gambling hall proprietors had their needs, too.

Almost everyone spent money freely, confident that the mines would deliver a continuous supply of gold. Their chief concern those days was the lack of efficiency shown by the newly established United States Postal Service, which in the fast-paced city was behaving like an awkward kind of dinosaur. Even though mail was the most important event in the lives of Californians, the service remained slow. Overworked, underpaid mail clerks, who had to sort and deliver the mail, must have dreaded those fortnightly arrivals of the mail steamers.

San Francisco now had board sidewalks. They allowed pedestrians to avoid the muddy streets churned by the hooves of horses. But heavy rains presented a new problem, driving out hundreds of rats that had made their homes under the wooden planking.

When the semaphore atop Telegraph Hill signaled a passenger ship was entering the harbor, whistles and bells would scream and toll the message. A volunteer fire engine drawn by prancing horses would come racing to the dock in case the ship burst into flame, as sometimes happened. Horse-drawn carriages of all kinds, including city buses, would appear and discharge their occupants. A band would strike up a lively tune.

As the ship unloaded, men and women began lining up in front of the post office and the express offices. Most express offices passed out the mail quickly. But the lines at the post office scarcely seemed to move. Sometimes it took two days for the clerks to sort out the mail. Throughout that time, people stood in line, afraid that if they left they would lose their place—unless they could hire someone to stand in for them. As the time wore on, tempers quickly frayed. Men began cursing and jostling one another as they tried to push to the front of the line. Fistfights broke out, frightened women wept.

Most of the express offices were far more efficient than the United States Postal Service not only at delivering mail but also at preparing and bagging outgoing mail and getting it to the steamer before it left port. Wells Fargo, with plenty of practice expressing mail in the east, was among the best of the San Francisco express agencies.

Wells Fargo agents were all carefully selected not just for their efficiency but also for their ability to treat all clients courteously no matter what their status in life or their nationality. After all gold was gold no matter who brought it and business was always business whether it came in big denominations or small ones.

Such unexpected courtesy astonished the Chinese businessmen of San Francisco. Used to being openly ridiculed and discriminated against for their shapeless clothes, their long thin braids, their strange language and customs, they found themselves suddenly being treated with the utmost

In contrast to the efficient express offices the United States Postal Service resembled an awkward dinosaur. Long lines of disgruntled clients in front of the understaffed post office was a common sight on every mail day.

After each fire, San Francisco was rebuilt even grander than before.

In the boom year of 1854 Wells Fargo, which was steadily expanding its services, moved into more spacious headquarters in Sacramento.

courtesy. Word spread throughout the large Chinese community in San Francisco and soon affluent Chinese businessmen in numbers were making the Wells Fargo office their bank of choice.

There was another reason for the whole-hearted endorsement of the Chinese. According to the ancient method of divination known as *feng-shui* (wind-water) the modest building which housed the Wells Fargo offices stood in one of the most favorable spots in the city. Such a location would surely attract the god of wealth who would take up his abode there. And anyone doing business in such an auspicious place would certainly be blessed.

chapter 21

Bust

FEW PEOPLE IN THE WEST STOPPED TO REALIZE how closely San Francisco's financial security was linked to that of the east. San Francisco merchants shipped most of their goods back east for sale, while eastern merchants sent their goods west for sale. The distance between the two coasts was so great that it took a long while for the transactions to be completed. This meant the merchants had to ask the banks for long-term loans to tide them over.

If for any reason the merchants could not dispose of their merchandise they would not be able to repay their debts and the banks that held the loans would suffer deficits. If there were many large deficits the banks would fail. Unknown to the San Franciscans this was exactly what was happening.

Cartoons of the time told the story of the 1855 panic. In the large central cartoon a malignant gnome stares down at men hauling on a rope attached to a bank that has fallen into San Francisco Bay. The Adams Company Bank is in the water, too, while Wells Fargo is "all right."

The town of Auburn, where John Q. Jackson managed the Wells Fargo branch office.

As 1854 drew to a close several large mercantile houses in the east began to fail because they had misjudged the public's demand for their products. Now they found their warehouses stocked with unsaleable goods. The banks that had made large loans to the owners of these houses were not being repaid. On top of this many banks both east and west were finding themselves in trouble because they had been investing heavily in stocks, which they discovered, too late, were utterly worthless.

In January of 1855 rumors began spreading that the Page, Bacon and Company bank, one of the largest in the east, with a branch bank in San Francisco, was looking unstable. The St. Louis branch of Page, Bacon and Company was having trouble meeting its New York obligations because a shipment of gold from San Francisco was late, and it was forced to suspend operation. Wary eastern depositors started withdrawing their money.

The news was headlined in the eastern papers. It was February 1855 when these papers arrived in San Francisco aboard the *Oregon* paddle steamer. The news hit San Francisco like a bombshell. February rains buffeted by a gale from the sea were lashing the city, and Montgomery Street was almost empty. But not for long! As the news got out, the street began to swarm with people of all kinds—miners in scruffy clothing, men in neat business suits and top hats, some with umbrellas. All were tramping through a swirl of mud, cursing, shouting threats, bellowing insults. There were a few women among them, their long dresses splattered with mud, rain-soaked bonnets wilting about their faces, others draped with Mexican shawls. They were weeping as they wandered through the oozing mud. Here and there a man was sobbing hysterically.

The crowds began to gather around Page, Bacon and Adams and Company, the two largest banks in the city. When the firms opened their doors, the crowd surged in. Page, Bacon's resources were quickly exhausted, and it had to close its doors.

Adams and Company was in trouble, too. Haskell apparently was no longer in charge of its operations. He had retired, leaving Isaiah C. Woods in charge. When Woods saw the crowds gathering at the doors of his bank, he began to call in the reserve deposits from all the

Wells Fargo office in Auburn where Jackson was employed as an agent.

branch offices, sending his messages by the local telegraph service. Each branch sent in its reserves and then closed its doors, despite the crowds of angry miners who were threatening to break into the company vaults.

The money from the branch offices was not nearly enough to save the day. By nightfall the mighty and reputable firm of Adams and Company had closed its doors for good. Rumors were abroad that hundreds of thousands of dollars had mysteriously disappeared from the bank vaults, along with its manager. Disguised as a woman, Woods had left on a ship bound for Australia.

Wells Fargo was also being deluged by depositors clamoring for their money. It, too, sent instructions to branch offices, but Wells Fargo ordered the branches to pay their local clients as long as the reserves held out. The agents, most of them young men, had a grueling experience ahead of them. In a long letter to his mother, Jackson, who was still agent at the Auburn branch, gave a picture of the problems he faced.

He began by telling how, on the night before the news came in, he had attended a party, staying up until four in the morning. He had expected to sleep late. Instead, according to his letter, "at eight o'clock I was awoke up by a telegraphic message to the effect that Adams and Company had failed and to prepare for a run."

As Jackson was hurrying to his office, he became aware of men brandishing guns around the branch office of Adams and Company. They were forcing the manager to open the branch vaults. They then rushed in to clean out all the cash.

Jackson's story continued: "The moment I reached the door, crowds were running toward the office. I knew that our funds would not meet all our outstanding drafts, certificates, etc. . . . The crowd was now furious and banking hours drawing nigh. . . . what was worse still I was alone in the office. . . . I saw no other plan but to open and let it go as far as it would."

With this decision Jackson opened the doors and began paying depositors. While he was doing this with a sinking heart, two or three of his friends showed up. They had heard of the run on the bank and had come to see if they could be of any help. Because they were influential men in the community, the crowd became somewhat assured by their presence. That gave the friends time to raise the necessary funds on their own, and payments went forward calmly until another telegraphic message delivered a second terrible blow: The San Francisco offices of

Twenty-three-year-old agent John Q. Jackson handled the clients who came for their money so calmly that he staved off panic at his office in Auburn.

Wells Fargo had suspended operations and closed its doors.

"This fell like a death knell to me," Jackson wrote, "but as far as this office was concerned I would weather it. . . . When the news was spread around the crowd began assembling, and pretty soon the paying out was lively. But as there seemed no lack of funds . . . all was quieted for the day . . . This morning [Saturday] I received a dispatch from the San Francisco office that their house would open on Monday next . . . I am in hopes we will go through the storm safely." Jackson then added with a note of satisfaction over a job well done, "This is the proudest time of my life."

Actually, Wells Fargo had closed its doors only long enough for its attorneys to review its books to find out how much reserve money it had available. On Sunday morning the bank published a notice in the local papers that read: "Wells Fargo and Company have completed a balance of their accounts and find . . . above every liability $309,105.23, and only ask of their friends a few days to convert some of these assets to resume payment."

Rain was still pouring down on San Francisco when Wells Fargo opened its offices on Tuesday. The city was seething with unrest. As the *Alta California* describes the scene: "The crowds which occupy Montgomery Street each hour of the day sufficiently demonstrate the fact that . . . the tension and fury at what the public saw as a betrayal might still erupt." What the paper feared was that with

Wells Fargo's prudent handling of its monetary affairs enabled it to expand, moving into the sumptuous offices in the Perrott building recently vacated by the failed Adams and Company.

tempers as high as they were a mob might gather to rampage through the city, burning banks and even lynching some suspected bank criminal.

And criminal it was, in the minds of many angry miners. They had seen their accumulated stash of gold, prudently banked for the long-awaited journey home, lost in a twinkling. According to one newspaper report, it was all because "the officers of these banks have been nothing more nor less than speculators . . . who have thousands of dollars of assets that are not now and never were worth a farthing."

The Forty-Niners Depart

THROUGH THE rest of 1855 and 1856 the recession continued to spread. In 1855, 197 businesses failed. There was a loss of 140 more in 1856. Some banks that had managed to hang on through 1855 had to close their doors, too. Most of the millionaires created by gold lost their money and their possessions, including their stately homes. They either left the city to look for work elsewhere or they joined the increasing number of unemployed, which included many miners who continued to drift down

Off went the miners by stagecoach or on foot to try the patience of Lady Luck at the rich Comstock Lode.

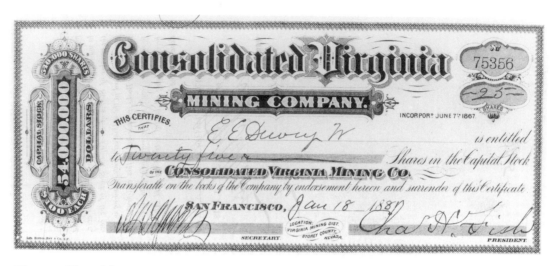

Shares like this one were sold by San Francisco companies to raise the necessary funds to finance deep-mining operations in Nevada.

from their now fruitless search for placer gold. Destitute and homeless, they spent their nights in doorways, in discarded packing boxes, or in any other small niche where they could find shelter from San Francisco rains and fogs and gales.

Saloons and gambling halls began serving free noon buffets where no one was turned away. But the seething undercurrent of rage continued to grow. Conditions were made even more dangerous by the rancorous rift between North and South in the east. It was now affecting Northern and Southern sympathizers in California. In San Francisco fiery speeches were followed by shootings. Vigilante groups again sprang up. After short one-sided trials two men were hanged. An uneasy quiet settled upon the city still reeling from the bank closures of 1855. Then in 1859 a familiar cry began echoing through the mining camps, cities, and towns of California: *Silver! Silver! Silver and gold, too! Rich deposits in the Comstock Lode!*

The Comstock Lode, as everyone knew, was just outside Virginia City, Nevada. It had delivered small amounts of gold and silver before, but now this cry was promising a bonanza of never-ending wealth.

So once again the trek began. Eastward over the mountains went the miners, some on foot, some on mules or horseback, a few in stagecoaches. The grimy, shaggy tide of men swept up through the passes of the Sierra Nevada. And as they went, they shouted, they quarreled, they drank and quarreled and laughed again. And they sang the ditty that had brought them to California in the first place, only this time with a change of words:

> *O Susanna! O don't you cry for me*
> *For I'm leavin' Californi-ay with my washbowl on my knee.*

And not one of them but was sure that this time Lady Luck was riding on his shoulder.

Along with the miners went some of the mining companies that were still operating a few of the deep mines in California. The mother lode of silver in Nevada would also have to be deep mined, and they had the equipment to do the job. They registered claims and were in business. Almost at once gold and silver began to make their way to San Francisco to be processed and minted. New instant millionaires were created, this time by silver, and new stately homes were built. New businesses opened up. The town had come to life again, a bustling metropolis.

Wells Fargo managers, deciding they needed more room, prepared to move to the spacious offices in the stone Perrott building across the street. This alarmed the Chinese. According to the ancient wisdom of *feng-shui* the building was located in a spot swarming with negative influences. As proof of their theory they had only to point

Comstock silver restored San Francisco's prosperity. And in the glow of regained affluence the panic of 1855 became just a painful memory.

to the fate that had befallen Adams Company and the Page, Bacon bank, once housed there.

A delegation of anxious Chinese elders finally approached Wells Fargo officials asking for permission to bring in a *feng-shui* master to cleanse the building of all evil influences. Since Wells Fargo didn't want to lose its faithful clientele it granted the Chinese permission. And the master went to work at once, performing numerous rites and reciting powerful incantations. He burned so much incense that the air turned blue with the fragrant smoke. At last he announced that the building had been thoroughly cleansed. It was now a fitting abode for the god of wealth. And Wells Fargo moved in.

Wells Fargo continued to expand, acquiring a whole line of Concord stagecoaches to create the well-known Wells Fargo express and passenger service that covered the West.

Epilogue

It's time now to close this account of an amazing era in American history. It brought thousands of travelers from everywhere to California, and in an astounding transformation turned San Francisco from a quiet frontier town into the most cosmopolitan city of its day.

Auburn, where once young John Quincy Jackson worked, still preserves its Old Town, where the old Wells Fargo office still stands. In Downieville visitors can see the gallows—or its replica—where Juanita died so gallantly for her honor that a town still does homage to her memory.

Even more haunting are the moldering ruins of forgotten mining camps hidden away in mountain fastnesses. They tell a lonely tale of ghosts who still walk there, dreaming of a lost home so far away. And there are the diaries and letters that tell their own poignant stories of the thousands of men who came out with such high expectations. Only one in twenty returned with the elusive treasure. No one knows how many others disappeared altogether, still lying in unknown, unmarked graves, tribute to the fickle cruelty of a golden dream.

Photograph & Illustration Credits

All photographs and illustrations courtesy of the Wells Fargo Archives except for the following:

The illustrations on pages 14, 15, 118, 119, and 131 courtesy of *Heritage of the West* by Charles Phillips (New York: Crescent Books).

The photographs and illustrations on pages 38, 50, 56, 75, 85, and 114 courtesy of the California State Library, California History section.

The illustration on page 49 courtesy of The New York Historical Society.

The illustration on page 58 and the photograph on page 87 courtesy of The Henry E. Huntington Library

The portrait on page 64 courtesy of The Southwest Museum.

The illustration on page 104 courtesy of the Library of Congress.

Bibliography

Axon, Gordon V. *The California Gold Rush.* New York: Mason/Charter, 1976.

Bean, Walton and James J. Rawls. *California: An Interpretive History.* Fourth Edition. Boston: McGraw, Hill, 1983.

Beebe, Lucius & Charles Clegg. *The Saga of Wells Fargo.* New York: E. P. Dutton & Co., Inc., 1949.

Boggs, Mae Bacon, ed. *My Playhouse Was a Concord Coach.* Oakland, CA: Howell-North Press, 1942.

Clappe, Louisa. *The Letters of Dame Shirley, California in 1851.* San Francisco, CA: The Grabhorn Press, 1933.

Caughey, John Walton. *California: History of a Remarkable State.* Englewood Cliffs, NJ: Prentice-Hall, 1982.

———. *Gold Is the Cornerstone.* Berkeley and Los Angeles, CA: University of California Press, 1948.

———. *Rushing for Gold.* Berkeley and Los Angeles, CA: University of California Press, 1949.

Downie, Major William. *Hunting for Gold.* San Francisco, CA: California Publishing Co., 1893.

Emanuels, George. *California Indians.* Walnut Creek, CA: Emanuels, self published, 1996.

Hutchinson, W. H. H. *California: Two Centuries of Man, Land & Growth in the Golden State.* Palo Alto, CA: American West Publishing Company, 1969.

Johnson, William Weber. *The Forty-niners.* New York: Time-Life Books, 1974.

Levy, Joann. *They Saw the Elephant: Women in California Gold Rush.* Hamden, CT: Archon Books, 1998.

Lewis, Oscar. *San Francisco: (Mission to Metropolis).* San Diego, CA: Howell-North Books, 1988.

———. *Sea Routes to the Gold Fields.* New York: Alfred A. Knopf, 1949.

———. *Sutter's Fort (Gateway to the Gold Fields).* Englewood Cliffs, NJ: Prentice-Hall, 1966.

Loomis, Noel. *Wells Fargo.* New York: C.N. Potter, 1968.

Manly, William Lewis. *Death Valley in '49.* CA: The Pacific Tree and Vine Company, 1894.

Marryat, Frank. *Mountains and Molehills.* New York: Harper & Bros., 1855.

McReynolds, Edwin C. *Missouri: A History of the Crossroads State.* Norman, OK: University of Oklahoma Press, 1962.

Nadeau, Remi. *Ghost Towns and Mining Camps of California.* Los Angeles, CA: Ward Ritchie Press, 1967.

Nevin, David. *The Expressmen.* New York: Time-Life Books, 1974.

Rohrbough, Malcolm J. *Days of Gold and the American Nation.* Berkeley and Los Angeles, CA: University of California Press, 1997.

Wilson, Neill Compton. *Treasure Express: Epic days of the Wells Fargo.* New York: Macmillan, 1936.

Woods, Daniel B. *Sixteen Months at the Gold Diggings: An account of a journey to the newly discovered gold regions of California.* New York: Harper & Brothers, 1851.

ARTICLES

Chandler, Robert J. "Henry Wells," "William George Fargo," and "Wells, Fargo & Company" in Larry Schweikart, ed. *Banking and Finance to 1913.* (New York: Facts on File Publications, 1990).

————. *Integrity Amid Tumult: Wells, Fargo & Co's Gold Rush Banking.* California History 70 (Fall 1991), pp. 258-77.

Excerpts from various diaries, letters, and news accounts from the Gold Rush years.

Gerlack, John and Sara Steck Melford. *Gold*, pp. 249-253. *The World Book Encyclopedia*, Vol. 8, 1996 Edition, World Book, Inc., Chicago.

Index